W9-CKM-755

1.00

1/00

THE
GEORGE ELIOT
MURDERS

By Edith Skom:

The Mark Twain Murders
The George Eliot Murders

THE
GEORGE ELIOT
MURDERS

EDITH SKOM

Delacorte Press

Published by
Delacorte Press
Bantam Doubleday Dell Publishing Group, Inc.
1540 Broadway
New York, New York 10036

The excerpts from the "Today's Thought" columns, by Reverend Paul S. Osumi, appeared in the *Honolulu Advertiser* and are reprinted with Reverend Osumi's permission.

Author's Note
This book is a work of fiction. Names, characters, places, and incidents are either the product of the author's imagination or are used fictitiously, and any resemblance to actual persons, living or dead, events, or locales is entirely coincidental.

Library of Congress Cataloging in Publication Data
Skom, Edith.
The George Eliot murders / by Edith Skom.
p.   cm.
ISBN 0-385-31228-8
1. Women detectives—United States—Fiction. 2. Women teachers—United States—Fiction. I. Title.
PS3569.K65G46   1995
813'.54—dc20   94-29791
                                                  CIP

Manufactured in the United States of America
Published simultaneously in Canada

May 1995

10 9 8 7 6 5 4 3 2 1

BVG

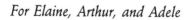

For Elaine, Arthur, and Adele

Acknowledgments

Special thanks to Shawn Coyne and Marjorie Braman, my editors, and Gail Hochman, my agent. You were great!

Mahalo to the wonderful staff of the fabulous Big Island resort, the Mauna Kea Beach. You inspired me to create the Royal Aloha.

For technical information on a variety of subjects, I would like to thank Robin Andelman, the Honorable William Bauer, Ron Cohn, George Cotsirilos, Irene Daria, Mary Dempsey, Jim Epstein, Scott Greenberg, Merle Gross, Joan Hall, Hugh Holton, Pat Kennedy, Robert Leroy, Amy Lubin, Thomas Morsch, Lillian Rubenstein, Bob Rubenstein, Dante Scarpelli, Alan Schwartz and Midtown Tennis Club, Steven Schwartz, Sharon Sharp, and Ben Spargo.

My thanks to Roslyn Schwartz who saw me off.

My without-you-I-couldn't-have thanks to Harriet Skom Meyer, Jean Smith, and Charles Yarnoff for seeing me through.

Most of all, my thanks to Joe Skom who continues to show graciousness in accepting my rejections of all his suggestions—except one. You are my favorite reader and best inspirer.

THE
GEORGE ELIOT
MURDERS

PROLOGUE

MIDWESTERN UNIVERSITY, EARLY DECEMBER

Beth Austin's adventure began in a setting linked more with re-
pose than excitement. The library periodicals room, during exam
week especially, provided a good escape. Its deep lounge chairs
were occupied now by students—some of them awake. Beth had
taken the one empty chair.

Among the piles of magazines on the carpet, a cover showing a
pristine beach and an inset photo of a Buddha caught Beth's eye.
After a guilty glance at her briefcase, bulging with ungraded exams, she began leafing through an article about the world's best
tropical resorts. Hawaii in the winter—fantastic! But travel during
her off quarter? She should stay on campus, continue her research,
prepare for the spring quarter. . . . She read on.

At the very top of the top-rated was one hotel. That this hotel was praised for its exquisite service, Beth expected. That its golf course was among the world's ten finest held little interest. But its gardens, its Asian art collection, its magnificent beach, its view-of-the-ocean tennis courts—these, *these,* made her sigh with longing.

"You've never been there? It's heaven. You'd love it," said her travel agent. "February? No way! Their clientele reserves a year ahead. Can't you make it later?"

"Later would be getting into spring quarter. Anyway, Sandy, what's the point of Hawaii in the spring?"

"I'll get back to you," said Sandy.

Outside Beth's office the campus was shrouded in its usual dismal gray. The sun, on a prolonged sabbatical, had not been sighted for weeks. Beth gazed out the window, watching, but not seeing, the dejected students who stumbled along, reading notes as they headed to exam rooms. She was imagining herself lying on a tropical beach. She was reading, but then the sun became too warm, so she threw off her robe and . . . Shaking her head as if to dissolve the image, she opened the first blue book.

Question 1: Explain what poet's work you most enjoyed reading this quarter and why.

"I liked Tennyson's 'Locksley Hall.' First, because I could relate to the blatant way he puts down material values. As an example . . ."

Beth's mind wandered. Couldn't this student relate to the lines about escape to "Breadths of tropic shade and palms in cluster, Knots of Paradise"?

The phone rang . . . Sandy! "Professor Austin, I'm so desperate! I need to talk to you about a paper."

Damn. The perfectionist student who had almost lived in her office this quarter. She swore silently and made the appointment.

The instant she put the phone down, it rang again. This *must* be Sandy. "Professor Austin? I'm from the *Prairie Gust.*" A reporter from Midwestern's student paper. He understood that Beth had unusually strong views on plagiarism. Not unusually strong, she told him, unless he saw something unusual in accepted professional ethics. Oh, of course not, that wasn't what he meant, he just wanted her thoughts about a recent lawsuit—the upshot being another appointment. She returned to the exam.

"Second, I could relate to how Tennyson depicts the end of a relationship. As an example of this . . ."

The phone. It would not be Sandy.

"You're in luck. They had a cancellation. And *you* get it because Bucky's an old pal of mine."

"Bucky?"

"He's the manager. But it'll cost you, Beth. The place isn't cheap."

"How much?" said Beth, sending silent thanks to her grandmother who had made larks like this possible.

Sandy told her how much.

Beth gasped.

"Beth? Can you hear me?"

A trust fund, but think of it as your mad money, Gran had said, and she had ordered Beth to be self-indulgent.

"Beth? Are you there?"

"I'm here. Just picking myself up off the floor." She made the reservation. Then, suddenly thinking of the February miracle of wearing shoes—not boots—of feet in contact with earth—not ice—she said, "One more thing, Sandy. Tell them I'm available for tennis."

Beth put a grade on the last exam and took the stack down to the English department. She opened the door to a horde of students, pleading for papers, begging for exams, like a mob of hungry peasants storming the Bastille.

"They're driving me nuts," said Dot, the department secretary. "Half of our darling faculty—naming no names—haven't even started grading papers yet, let alone exams. Come on, I'll give you some coffee." She dragged Beth into her office, kicking the door shut behind her.

"Three glorious weeks in Hawaii, huh?" said Dot. "Well, well. And you're going alone? What about your FBI agent? Where is that guy, anyway?"

"Gil's out of town," said Beth. "And he is not *my* FBI agent, Dot. He doesn't belong to me—and I don't belong to him. You're acting as if Gil is my Casaubon."

"What the hell is a kissawbong?"

"Casaubon—he's a creepy character in *Middlemarch*."

"*Middlemarch*? One of those books like *Midlife Sex*?" Dot said. "Can I borrow it? . . . What's so funny?"

"Great . . . guess . . ." Beth choked out between giggles. Then, getting herself under control, she said, "Middlemarch is a place, Dot, in a Victorian novel by George Eliot—set in England in the early nineteenth century."

Dot's eyes glazed. "Oh, *literature*—forget it. Listen, about Hawaii. You'll have a ball, darling. You'll guzzle those rum-and-pineapple drinks with the little umbrellas, you'll lay around on the beach, you'll meet a guy—"

"I'm going away to escape winter—not to meet anyone."

"You'll meet a guy, you'll do the hula with him. . . . Oh, and you have to get mixed up in a murder."

"Mixed up in a murder! Why would you say a thing like that?"

"How else will you meet a guy?"

CHAPTER

1

Looming white against the dawn sky, the hotel looked like a fifties liner. Smooth, sleek, powerful horizontal lines, it could have been the S.S. *United States* in its heyday. Its promenade deck was the graceful walk that swept south to the jogging trail and north to the luau courtyard, its sports deck the higher walk that led south to the golf course and north to the tennis pavilion.

From the bay side, the ship effect was even more striking. The hotel seemed to be coasting over the dark water, not on an aimless cruise from port to port, but crossing the ocean to one destination, taking its passengers on a glorious voyage.

At the front of the building, where palm trees crisscrossed a grassy circle, surrounded by a broader circle of driveway, a small motorcade emerged in the lush, greeny light. A smart little orange truck, carrying golf bags, zoomed toward the pro shop. White trucks, loaded with Igloo watercooler refills, darted off to the jogging trail. At the back, along what the guidebooks called the most beautiful curve of beach in the Hawaiian Islands, machines smoothed the grass and raked the sand, while beach boys cranked up umbrellas, skimmed the pool, swept the steps.

The sky lightened, and the day's first jogger appeared. He walked to a palm tree, devoted himself to stretching exercises, then loped toward the trail.

Inside the building, the reservations manager shook her head. "*Moi lepo*—dirty," she said, and sent a bellboy off to clean his shoes. The tennis assistant stopped at the front desk to leave presents for arriving guests, then went to look over the day's requests for games.

Up on the floors, waitresses in flowered muumuus pushed cartloads of macadamia nut waffles, pineapple pancakes, lox and bagels, and knocked on doors, sending out the sweet sound of "Aloha! Room Service."

It was seven o'clock on a February morning at the Royal Aloha on the island of Hawaii.

CHAPTER
2

TUESDAY

Some guests were still asleep, some were leaving their rooms for the beach, or tennis, or golf, and some were just finishing breakfast, lingering over yesterday's paper, not minding that, as usual, today's paper was late. Reading news from two days ago made them feel pleasantly removed from the world's dilemmas, just as being at the Royal made them feel pleasantly removed from home, safe from the problems they had left behind.

High up, on eight, the guest in 803 was deep in a phone conversation.

"It's so crazy," she was saying. "Can you really wear a leotard in a New York summer?"

She was a tall woman, not old, but not so young either, early forties perhaps. Something about the way she had tied it made the hotel robe—a voluminous *yukata*—look distinctive, as she was herself. Sculptured black hair cut geometrically around the forehead, thin, tense face. "Or a Chicago summer?" she said, carrying the telephone out to the lanai.

"What? Versatile, sure, but it's like bundling women up in a snowsuit. Then take off the jacket and every bulge—hey, Dale! I see a whale! . . . Of course. That's why I always ask for the ocean side."

"You want details? Where are you? I mean, can anyone hear you? . . . No, I am not paranoid. Last year Addie C. was knocked off but good."

"I'm not talking about a sleeve or a collar. I mean line for line. *Five bodies,* Dale, five of her bodies on the showroom rack. I mean, the chutzpah was so colossal . . . colossal!"

"They don't call it copying, darling. They call it interpreting. Tell me! There is no decency in this industry. *I'd* never do it."

"No, not a thing she can do. Oh, naturally if she had won an award—that would be murder."

"Listen, Dale, it's a gorgeous group." She shooed a bird away from the table, speared a wedge of pineapple, and sat down, putting her feet on the rail. "They're minimalist. . . . No, no—closer to the body, but classy . . . No, darling, not like Ralph, not so constricting."

"For sure they've got glamour. Why do you think I'm calling it LeDND? Get it? . . . No, no. L.E.—Lunette, Eleanor. Definitely Not Dowdy."

"Very simple, very elegant, like bedrooms in thirties movies. Wait till you see my favorite—the Harlow."

"Oh"—she hesitated—"I've been playing with it since Pratt."

"Morninghills is going to do a whole boutique—" Eleanor stopped mid-reach for another pineapple wedge. "I hope they're going to do a boutique. Listen, do you have the *Times*? Naturally, but it's always a day late here."

"Oh, God," she said a moment later. "We need Morninghills—they're our biggest account. But I can't afford to ship—not without money. I've got a payroll to meet. And Jerry said thirty-five thousand dollars' worth of fake fur came in yesterday. Oh, God, I don't know what to do. If they'd just go into Chapter Eleven, then . . . *Come in!* . . . Dale? Hang on. Thought I heard someone outside."

She put down the phone, walked barefoot over the carpet. On the tile was an envelope. She opened it, read the contents, then ran to the door. Wild-eyed, she scanned the atrium, seeing only a few people in bathing suits and robes, and children tearing back and forth.

"Dale? . . . I can't talk now. No, nothing's the matter . . . just . . . I'll talk to you later."

She stood looking down at the beach, watching a cat whose color, chameleonlike, matched the sand. It slipped a paw into a crab hole, made its snatch, and disappeared.

Then she moved back into the room, staggered to the bed, and lay there, staring upward.

CHAPTER

3

"The newspapers are late this morning," said the waitress. "They took all of them off the plane in Maui." She unplugged the toaster, put it inside the cabinet, folded the yellow tablecloth, and put it on top the cart. "I'll drop one off as soon as they come in."

"Anytime," said Beth. A gust of air as the door opened, and she caught a glimpse of Reeboks under the waitress's muumuu, signal of a workaday world she wanted to forget. She stretched out on a lounge, exulting in the sounds of sprinklers and birds.

Behind her was the supersnow that had paralyzed Chicago, and had left in its wake a Midwestern campus suffering from a deeper-than-usual February depression. Partly it was the sheer effort of getting from one place to another, partly the unremitting gray-whiteness of the landscape, the only relief a plucky FREE SNOW sign atop one of the grimy mountains created by removal trucks. No wonder the passengers had broken into applause—and she had joined them—when the plane took off from O'Hare. Sixteen hours and one plane change later, when they landed in Kona, she had wanted to kiss the grass.

She thought about the drive that followed. Half asleep, she had stared out at mile upon mile of graffiti-covered lava rock. Then the limousine had taken a sharp turn off the highway and pulled up to a gatehouse. The passengers' names were given, they were waved on, and she had felt a jet-lagged shock of delight as they entered the enchanted grounds of the Royal Aloha.

Even her room spoke of perpetual summer. Framed seashells on the walls. An orchid plant atop a lacquered chest. Bright batik covering the deep rattan chairs. Something skidded under the door. She padded over and picked up the daily activities calendar for the Royal Aloha on the island of Hawaii.

On the lanai she looked over the calendar, at once deciding that she would not take a helicopter to the volcano, that she would not visit a macadamia nut factory, that she would not take scuba diving lessons.

Far below, a whale tossed playfully in the ocean and surfers boogie-boarded the waves. On the beach, mothers and fathers—well-heeled mothers and fathers, thought Beth—carried sand toys, toddlers trailing after them. On the grass, an aerobics class kicked and lunged to a rock-and-roll beat. But the lounge chairs, spread with purple towels, were what appealed. She could see a spot in the shade that seemed meant for her. Not yet, no hurry.

She closed her eyes, listening, but not really, to a soft jumble of conversation from surrounding rooms. Someone making dinner reservations—she must think about that. Someone calling home to ask about the horses—the storm in the East must be as fierce as the one in Chicago. She thought about the leak in her apartment ceiling, then put it firmly out of her mind. More voices floated up: "Where'sthesunscreendidyoubringthecamera?"

"Or a Chicago summer?" Beth opened her eyes. A cheerful New York voice, so clear it must be just below.

She lay there, listening unashamedly. *"Five bodies,* Dale, five of her bodies on the showroom rack."* Not serial murder, Beth realized almost at once—"the chutzpah was so colossal"—but idea-stealing. Colossal chutzpah indeed, Beth thought, whether the thief was in fashion or academia. She detested plagiarism in any form.

But why, she wondered a few minutes later, had Eleanor ended the conversation so abruptly? And why had Eleanor's voice suddenly lost its confidence? She sounded as if the bottom had dropped out of her world. Did it have anything to do with what Eleanor had heard outside the door? . . . Oh forget it—Beth opened her book.

After some time she paused, thinking about the fantastic contrasts that came of reading *Middlemarch* at a tropical resort. Miss Dorothea Brooke, walking through the woods, excitedly contemplating marriage to an intellectual clergyman—and several stories below, bikinied bods, running the beach. What would the Reverend Casaubon think of the aerobics class, gyrating wildly in full view of the world? She sighed. The good thing about rereading *Middlemarch* was that she always discovered something she hadn't noticed before. The bad thing was that she had to watch Dorothea make the same mistake. Still, this was exactly what she wanted to do, just lie here and read George Eliot.

The telephone rang.

Could Beth fill in for a tennis round-robin this afternoon?

"I'd love to."

CHAPTER
4

All the pleasant business of a tennis afternoon was going on at the courts. People chatting, waiting to play. People who had finished playing having a drink. From the spotlight court, where the pro was hitting, came the satisfying ping of ball meeting racket.

"Come on, Zip. Quit playing customer's tennis."

The pro grinned. "Want to take over?"

"Nah," the heckler said good-humoredly. "Everyone deserves a second chance." He was a pudgy man, wearing regulation whites and red tennis shoes that underscored his body like a punch line. His wife—she must be his wife, they were sitting so far apart— was California trim and tan. Capable-looking, Beth thought, as if she had chaired many a benefit. "Now, dear," she was saying, "don't be a rabble-rouser."

Beth went to the desk and gave her name to Zip's assistant.

"Oh," said the benefits woman, overhearing. "You're in our round-robin. Aren't you nice to fill in? I'm Winifred Delorio—"

"But you can call her Doc," said the pudgy man, getting up from his chair. "And I'm Twinky. Where you from, Beth? . . . Oh, where they're having all the weather. Here with your husband?" Twinky quickly established that Beth was alone. "What do you . . ." He looked up at a man making his way to the table. "Well, Burt, did you unpack?"

Burt, dignified, ponderous, looked the way people always assumed scholars looked, but did not. He carried a book and tennis rackets for two. "Everything shipshape," he said. "If you think about it, unpacking is like crossing the *t*'s and dotting—"

"Hang on a sec, Burt," said Twinky. "You haven't met our—"

"Oh, sorry." Burt looked abject. "Rude of me. I'm Burton Breneman, and this— Where is she? Oh there you are. This is Suzy. My wife," he added, somewhat reluctantly.

Ambling toward them was a woman with a roly-poly figure and a face like a children's book illustration, snub-nosed with Raggedy Ann features. "Hi," she said. "Oh God . . ." strewing an armload of fashion magazines on the terrace. Muttering about why she had to bring that junk in the first place, Burt picked up the magazines.

"Here's your partner, Beth," Zip's assistant called. "This is Link—" The last name was lost in a shout from the pro's court. Leaning against the desk was a dark-haired man in worn tennis clothes. He had a clever face, and sad-comic eyes. He walked over, and there were first-name introductions all around.

"Say, Beth," said Twinky. "What's your rank?" She hesitated. Should she say her tennis was rusty? "Are you an A, B, or C?" Twinky persisted.

"Clearly an A," said Link, "and she's stuck with me."

But they were missing their last couple, someone said. Where were Bruce and Carlotta?

"Yoo-hoo! Yoo-hoo!"

A golf cart zoomed down from the walk above, just cleared their table, and pulled up neatly next to them. Out jumped a gray-haired man, movie-star handsome—Bruce, Beth assumed—and a fabulous-looking woman, very tall with a big sweep of blond hair. She must be Carlotta.

"Well, a-lo-*hah*!" Screams of delight, a scramble of people jumping up, hugs and kisses.

"Wondered where you were!"

"How was your year?"

"Your hair is lighter—I love it! Do you think I . . . ?"

"Played any lotto lately?"—Twinky to Bruce.

"Put on a few pounds in the breadbasket?"—Bruce to Twinky.

"Makes me think of my City High reunion," Link told Beth.

"Or a Camp Bluebird get-together?" she said.

"Oh stop," said Doc. "We can catch up later. Beth and Link, let me introduce Bruce and Carlotta Howard. Our missing players are here at last."

"Our round-robin," said Burt, turning to Beth and Link, "is somewhat unusual. Think of a directors' meeting, when they have a long agenda, but only—"

"Hang on a sec," said Twinky, and he quickly explained that the round-robin consisted of two preliminary rounds and a final. "And the winners get . . . Hey, Zip!" he called to the pro, a very tall man with a powerful build, and a look of confidence about him. He came beaming up to them, exchanging kisses and handshakes with Bruce and Carlotta.

"Meet Zip Heinz," said Twinky, "the all-time great head tennis pro."

Zip laughed, a deep bellow. "What are you after?"

"What have you provided for the winners of this important event?"

"I have provided," he said, "a handsome set of Royal Aloha glasses."

Cheerful howls of derision, mock moans of "not again." But all in fun, and for some reason, Beth thought of Eleanor Lunette, alone in her room.

"How about loser pays everyone's hotel bill?" Twinky was saying.

"You'll never see four men play harder," said Carlotta.

CHAPTER 5

"Aloha! Room Service!"

"Come in," Eleanor called from the bed.

The waitress unlocked the door, came in with her tray, and looked around as if expecting to see other people. "You ordered three mai tais?"

"Yes. You can take back those chips. Just put it here." She motioned to the bedside table.

Before the waitress was out the door, she had finished the first drink. She started the second, then picked up the letter again.

CHAPTER 6

"You stay in the alley, Suzy," Burt said. "I'll cover the rest."

Infuriating, Beth thought, but Suzy made no comment, and the game proceeded. Burt played like a gentleman, saving his hard serve for Link, calling all the close ones in their favor. Suzy made it a Mad Hatter's tennis game.

"Where's the third ball?" she asked, just as Burt was serving, throwing him off so much he double-faulted. "Oh, my God," she said in the middle of a point. "I forgot one hand."

"Suzy"—Burt ran for the ball—"I—don't—know—what—you're—talking—about."

"My nail polish. Look." She held up a hand.

Beth waited, but the explosion from Burt never came. And Suzy continued to play her own way, paying attention intermittently. There was one surprise. When she happened to connect at the net, she knew just how to angle the ball for a winner.

"Great shot, Suzy," said Link. "Right down the middle."

"Isn't that the highest percentage shot?" she said proudly.

"Okay with you if I serve first?" said Link. Beth nodded. She would have resented it as condescending politeness, if he'd let her start.

Link was very good indeed, with a wicked forehand drive and great volleys. He was also a congenial partner. "Perfect," he said, when Beth missed an easy forehand. "Now he'll think it's a weakness—and you'll put the next one away."

The result was that Beth played better than she could. She felt exhilarated, in tune with her partner, in love with where she was, gazing between points at the sparkling ocean.

Burt played well, but could not overcome Suzy's game. "Suzy," he said, as they came off the court, "you can't leave the alley open like that. It's . . . it's like putting your feet too close to the fire." Suzy gazed at Burt, nodding her head and playing the obedient wife. Beth had seen that same look of false concentration before, in the classroom.

The round against Twinky and Doc was much closer. Twinky had a tough spin serve he didn't mind using against Beth. Then he would show off, returning the ball behind his back or between his legs, occasionally hitting out. He could afford some misses because he had a fine partner. "She's mean," said Twinky approvingly, as Doc smashed one away.

Between Doc's smash and Twinky's spin, they were losing. "I know we can beat them," Link told Beth as they changed sides. "Just block his serve and we'll move into the net and smash back."

The turning point came when Beth returned Twinky's serve with a perfect down-the-liner.

"Oh, yes," said Doc. "I'd keep that one in the repertoire."

"Out," said Twinky.

"I'm sure it was on the line . . . dear."

"And I know it was out."

Ignoring Twinky's glare, Doc said they should play it over—
which they did, and lost the point. Twinky stalked back to the
baseline, head down, belly forward. A few points later, he double-
faulted. "Dammit, Doc! You moved and distracted me."

Beth tensed for an explosion—this time from Doc.

"Sorry, dear," Doc said from the net.

"What's the matter with these people?" Link muttered to Beth.
She looked at him questioningly. "No conflict," he said. "Bunch
of Stepford spouses."

When it was clear they were losing, Twinky became a buffoon,
making slapstick dives, poaching and missing on shots Doc could
have put away. "What a character," said Doc, looking embarrassed.

"At least I'm creative," said Twinky. "Well," putting an arm
around Doc, "we showed them plenty of aloha."

So they were in the finals, against the glamour couple. Bruce
changed to a fresh T-shirt. Carlotta pulled a turban over her
sweep of hair. The others ran to get drinks, then pulled up chairs
to watch from the shaded terrace.

"Take it easy," said Link, when Bruce served hard to Beth.

"Sorry," he said. "I can't control it," though this seemed unlikely. Bruce was the best man they had played—always got to
the ball, but never looked as if he was running that hard.

Carlotta was a bouncy player, up-to-date on the latest sounds
and moves, grunting as she hit, shimmying when she received.
When it was her turn to serve, she stood at the baseline and called
out in her high, clear voice, "FBI?"

Beth jumped, thinking of an FBI agent she knew very well indeed.

"FBI?" said Link.

"First Ball In," Carlotta said condescendingly.

"But of course," said Link. "And people who say FBI," he muttered, "they'd none of them be missed."

"I've got a little list," said Beth. She and Link were a team now, more than holding their own—until the next time Carlotta served. Beth looked up. Bruce had left the alley and was squatting right in the center.

Beth hit a crosscourt return. Bruce put it away. And the next. And the next. "When he's in the middle like that," she told Link, "I don't know where to hit. What's he doing?"

"They're playing Australian style," said Link. "It's distracting, but the thing to do is not worry about where he's going. Just aim for those Polo socks."

The next time Beth received, she hit directly at Bruce—for a winner.

There was a loud clap. Beth looked at the terrace. Her cheerleader, sitting apart from the reunion group, was a rotund, white-haired man, with an Alfred Hitchcock profile. He gave her a big grin.

At 6–6 a tiebreaker was called.

The score went back and forth. 9–8. 11–10. The court was in full sun now. Carlotta had ceased grunting and shimmying. Even Bruce looked wilted. He hit another hard serve at Beth, and Link gave him a meaningful stare. "Soon," he said under his breath, "we *will* have conflict."

"Forget it," she said. "I like challenge."

The score was 15–14. Beth was serving. She glanced at the Hitchcock man. He smiled encouragingly. She threw the ball up, made good contact—Bruce looked bewildered.

She had aced him!

Applause from the reunion group. The Hitchcock man clasped his hands over his head in a boxer's victory gesture.

Link moved as if to kiss Beth's cheek, stopped short, kissed her hand. Then they ran to shake hands with Carlotta and Bruce.

Carlotta pulled off her turban and shook out her magnificent hair. "Oh well," she said. "We have three sets of glasses at home. Where are we having dinner?"

CHAPTER
7

The telephone rang and rang.

"This is Housekeeping. Can we make up your room now?"

"Later," snapped Eleanor Lunette. She fumbled with the receiver, finally found the Room Service button. "Where the hell are those drinks?"

Then she stumbled into the bathroom, ripped the letter in pieces, and flushed them down the toilet.

CHAPTER
8

T he competition over, they all—even Carlotta and Bruce—
thanked Beth and Link for joining them, and congratulated Zip's
assistant on finding such great players.

Now drinks had been brought, chairs pulled in a circle. Idly
they watched the games in surrounding courts and talked vacation talk.

"Beth," Suzy said lazily, "aren't you from where they have all
the Miles van der Rohes?"

"*Mies,*" said Burt. "Mies van der Rohe."

"Miles sounds better," Suzy said.

"Near Chicago, actually," Beth said quickly, because she
thought Suzy minded more than she appeared to. "Vinetown."

"Watch your English, everyone," said Twinky. "She's a professor—on leave from Midwestern. Link," he said, "I didn't get your
last name."

"Lowenstein." Link took a big swallow of beer.

"You're not *the* Lincoln Lowenstein!" Suzy jumped up in her chair. "You are! Oh, my God, this man writes the *most* wonderful books. *Made in Heaven. To Seek a Newer World*—I just loved the grandmother in that one. The way she stood up to that cossack! And her granddaughter was just like her. The way she ran that magazine! Now what's your new one?"

"*By Faith Alone,*" said Link.

"It's about someone with amnesia, isn't it? I just love stories about amnesia. I can't wait to start it. Beth—you must have read his books!"

Beth hesitated. "I've seen them," she said, picturing a rack of supermarket paperbacks with gold-embossed covers.

"Don't put her on the spot," said Link. "Henry James, I'm not. And Beth reads literature. Right, Beth?"

"I'm pretty much stuck in the nineteenth century—Jane Austen, George Eliot"—she paused—"Mark Twain."

"How did Mark Twain get in there?" Link asked.

"He jumped off a raft and turned up one day at Midwestern. Said he wanted to see life off the Mississippi."

"Sounds intriguing," said Link. "Was he tired of roughing it?"

"Let's get back to the here and now," said Twinky. "Link, how do you account for your success?"

"What do you mean?" said Suzy. "He writes super books!"

"No, no—it's not the books," said Link. "The secret"—he paused dramatically—"is double consonants."

Double consonants? They asked what on earth he meant.

"Frederick Forsyth, Sidney Sheldon—double consonants do it every time. Norman Mailer just misses. If he'd change his name to Morton, he'd hit the bestseller list for months."

"But . . ." Suzy looked puzzled. "How about Judith Krantz? . . . Oh, I see. You're kidding. Anyway, I want to have my picture taken with you."

"Ma'am." Link swept off his tennis cap. "I'd be honored. So," he said, "you guys have been coming here awhile?"

Oh forever, they said, and we've had some great times, and how long was it, anyway?

"Year ten, exactly," said Burt.

"Tell us about the great times," said Beth.

"Yeah," said Link. "Tell us."

Link wanted to put them in a book, Twinky said knowingly, and did they have material for him. "Remember, Carlotta, when you asked if it was legal for me to purposely lob into the sun?" He imitated Carlotta's voice. " 'I can't see the ball when he does that!' "

"Knock it off, Twink," she said. "I'd just started."

"Now stop picking on Carlotta," said Doc.

"Yeah, sure," said Twinky. "But these are the guys"—nodding toward Bruce and Carlotta—"to put in a book."

Beth wondered if Link was thoroughly tired of hearing that remark, but his face showed only friendly interest.

"You're looking," Twinky went on, "at lifestyles of the rich and famous. These guys pick up and go to Paris the way other people go to . . . to . . ."

"Peoria?" said Beth.

"Peoria—that's good."

"We'd do even more if we could swing it," said Carlotta.

"My God," Suzy said wistfully. "What would you do that you don't do already?"

"Easy—all the dresses I want without Bru grumbling."

"A Mercedes, 500 SL," said Bruce.

"A house in London," said Carlotta, "a chalet in Gstaad. A *long* stay in Venice—the Cipriani. You know how much that place is? It makes the Royal look like chicken feed."

"I hear Illinois has a big lotto jackpot," said Twinky.

A silence—not a comfortable one, Beth thought. Bruce and Carlotta looked . . . what? Embarrassed? Annoyed?

"Uh-oh. That's a little short. You were greedy." Zip's voice carried from the far court.

"Well, let's see what happens," said Bruce, addressing the whole group as much as Carlotta. "I'm into a deal for— Hey, Zip, how did that tip work out last year?" he shouted, as if hoping the pro would confirm his shrewd business instincts.

Zip held up a hand and stood talking with his student. They heard him make plans to have dinner later in the week. Then he came over, winked at Beth, and threw himself into a chair. "It worked out great," he said. "I could always use another. Got any more?"

Bruce said that he might. "Now's the time to buy—when everything's in the toilet."

Beth studied Zip's face as he talked eagerly with Bruce about the market. Who did he remind her of? She puzzled a moment, and then forgot it. She stretched, loving the ocean breeze. The afternoon was pure magic.

"Look at that," Carlotta said suddenly.

A raucous group of straw-hatted men and women emerged from the pro shop—oohing, aahing, pointing, milling around the tennis desk. Zip went over and introduced himself.

"Say, how do you get a game around here?"

Carlotta looked with disdain at the questioner, a potbellied man in a WELCOME, CUTORA DEALERS T-shirt. "That's the kind of riffraff they're getting here now," she said. "Before I play tennis with him—or those other hicks!"

Doc said she had seen them in the lobby when they checked in.

"I can imagine, darling," said Carlotta. " 'You mean there's no TV?' "

If they started catering to groups, Burt said, they were going to ruin the place. "I told Bucky—it's like you're shooting yourself in the foot."

"It's started already," said Carlotta. "They made us wait one hour at check-in, and then the girl showed us a room over the parking lot! Well, I mean! We went right back down. Bucky, I said —they have someone else in my room."

"*Your* room, Carlotta?" said Twinky.

"We've always had 9334—with the double sinks and extra closets."

Doc asked if they'd straightened it out.

"You'd better believe it," said Bruce, a grin of satisfaction lighting his handsome face.

"The Royal," said Carlotta, "is on the skids."

Beth looked around at the manicured lawns, the beautifully kept courts, and listened to Carlotta spew out grievances—no fruit basket or champagne in the room when they arrived, recycled anthurium flowers on the breakfast table. "And the service! Well, I mean! Last year—I timed it—they made us wait one hour and fifteen minutes in the Raffia. I told Bucky."

Carlotta's discourse unleashed more gripes. "Ran out of umbrellas at the beach. . . . Raffia's looking seedy—need to redo it. I told Bucky . . . they better have fixed up the jogging trail. . . . Last year . . . fitness stations all torn up. . . . I told Bucky . . . I told Bucky . . ."

"Who's Bucky?" Link asked.

"Bucky?" They looked surprised. "Bucky's the manager."

On they went, talking darkly of the competition—the Ritz was going up, the Four Seasons. "Zip," someone asked, "what's the occupancy?"

"The house is full to the top," he said cheerfully.

"Well, they'd still better wise up," said Carlotta. "You can tell Bucky—the Cutora dealers of America don't know from fifty-dollar tennis lessons."

"I don't care," said Suzy. "The day I stop coming here I'll be seven feet under."

Everyone laughed. "Six, Suzy. Six feet under."

"Hey, Zip," said Bruce. "Can I get a lesson on my serve tomorrow?"

He needed it, Twinky said, as Zip went to the desk, waited while a guest used the phone to call home for messages, then checked his book. "How about ten?" he said.

"Too much sun," said Bruce. "How about eight?"

Zip said sorry, but that time was taken.

"I'll buy the time," said Bruce. "How much for eight A.M. for the next two weeks?"

Zip laughed his deep bellow, but he looked a touch sullen. "You know I can't book prime time two weeks in advance."

"For chrissake!" Bruce picked up a stray ball and slammed it into the shrubbery. "We drop thirty or forty grand every time we come!"

"Hang on a sec," said Twinky. "That's not the old aloha spirit."

There was a soft, hooting sound, like a muted trumpet.

"There goes the conch!" With cries of "I've got a massage," and "Late for my pedicure," and admonitions for Link and Beth to play with them again, the group went off, Suzy trailing magazines, Twinky breaking into a run. Someone asked Twinky what was the rush. "My daily good-luck shot," he said. "Gotta rub the Buddha's belly." His red shoes flew up and down as he jogged up the steps toward the main building.

Link and Beth followed slowly. "You seem preoccupied," he said.

"Just trying to get the names straight," said Beth. "I'm making mental notes on everyone—like the first day of class."

Link asked how that worked.

"You really want to know? Okay—I draw a diagram because

students usually sit in the same place around the seminar table. Then I jot down names, characteristics."

"For example?"

"Oh . . . long, dark hair . . . classy-looking—"

"That's Doc."

"Very good . . . Chubby, jokey . . . the class clown."

"Hang on a sec," said Link. "That's not the old aloha spirit."

Beth laughed. "Excellent. Next—glasses? Dignified?"

"That's Burt. Typical prelaw. How about Suzy?" and when Beth hesitated, "A little dizzy?" Link suggested.

Beth shook her head. "She's not so dizzy, really. Suzy is . . . the class darling. Everyone loves her because she sees something to admire in everyone, especially her boyfriend, Burt."

"Then who's Carlotta? The class glamour girl?"

"She is glamorous, but . . ." Beth thought a moment. "Carlotta is the class mourner."

"What in God's name is that?"

" 'You mean,' " Beth wailed, " 'I've got to write a ten-page paper?' The mourner expresses the fears of the entire class."

Link threw back his head and laughed. "Great concept," he said. "Can I use it?"

"As long as you cite me."

"I'll dedicate the book to you. How's that?"

She stared. His eyes were so blue, blue as . . . the wrapper of the *New York Times,* and that, she thought, brings me back to reality. "Just a footnote will do," she said. "Let's see . . . we haven't done Bruce."

At the courts, the tennis assistant was on the phone. "Right. Court Five . . . B players . . . No, strong B's . . . I'm *sure* they'll give you a good game. And that," she said, putting down the receiver, "takes care of tomorrow. Hey, old Zip"—she ruffled his hair—"do I see a streak of gray in those curls? What's your problem? Couldn't give old Bru the time he wanted? Put him in the computer!"

Zip shook his head. "Some people don't have a clue as to how to have a vacation. It's so fuckin' amazing just to be alive—to be in Hawaii—to be at the Royal—and they still don't know— Well, hello. How are things?"

"Peachy keen," said the assistant golf pro. "So, here it is," he said, as he stood, hands on hips, looking at the golf cart. "Some day, some wonderful day, I'm going to tell Brucie and Carlotta exactly—"

"Remember," the tennis assistant sang out. "Your smile . . ."

"Will travel a mile," finished the golf pro with a mocking falsetto. "You know what the Platinum Couple did this time? They just waltzed up to the pro shop, found a cart with a key in it, and took off—not a word to anyone. What would you call that?"

"What would I call that?" said Zip. He paused a moment. "I would call it colossal chutzpah."

"Mr. Bruce Howard. Room 9334. Showed colossal chutzpah," said the assistant. "Put it in the computer!"

CHAPTER
9

In the atrium, twittering birds played their dusk game, making daring swoops from lofty branches down to the floors below—a precipitous drop. The high railing along the atrium corridor was there obviously to protect against a fall.

Beth took the stairs down the nine flights and found herself in the central courtyard, where a colorful macaw was practicing acrobatics. Dinnergoers stopped to watch the show, then drifted on. She was wondering what direction to take for the main dining room, when the elevator door opened, and out stepped the Hitchcock man, wearing a red jacket, bright blue trousers, and a plaid tie in sunset colors. His face was serious, until he saw her. Then he lit up. "Hello, tennis star! Nice to see you! I'm Sig Winterfield."

"Hi . . . Sig." She almost said "Hitch," because up close—the full face, the mischievous look—the resemblance held. She introduced herself and thanked him for being their cheerleader.

"Hot ziggety! You played a great game, Beth. Where's your husband?"

"He's not . . . I'm not . . ."

"Whatever. His bad judgment is my good luck. Come have a drink with me." But she had a reservation. "Oh, not there. You should have your first dinner in the Raffia—with me." But her reservation? "I'll take care of it," Sig said grandly.

Taking her arm, he guided her down the flagstoned corridor, past shops displaying Asian antiques and menswear in absurd colors, past an orchid-surrounded pool, where improbably large goldfish swam in circles. Across the pool, lights were on in the windowed offices, and a cleaning crew was at work. Through one window, she could see a man bent over a cluttered desk. "Bucky's working late," said Sig. The illustrious Bucky!—screened by a plant. She could see only a full head of neatly-parted dark hair.

Then they were outside on a hill overlooking the ocean. In the distance, far beyond the bay, the lights of Maui sparkled. Surely the winking stars above were much closer. "Beautiful, isn't it?" said Sig. "The first night my wife and I were here we stood in this spot and she said, 'I think I'm in heaven.' "

The cocktail terrace was in a holiday mood. Groups chattered animatedly and nibbled *pupus* from tiny grills. Couples held hands and listened to the music. The instant they stepped in, a sturdy, muumuued waitress charged up to Sig, arms open wide. "Here come the judge!" she whooped.

"Aloha, Betty!" They hugged energetically. "You been behaving yourself?"

"You're damn tootin'. But not you"—smiling at Beth. "Saved your table," she said, guiding them to a ringside spot. "Your usual, Mr. W.? And the lady?"

Beth thought of a mai tai, but Sig said too potent while she still had jet lag, and suggested Betty's concoction, Kohala Dream. "Betty, I want to have dinner with this young lady in the Raffia, and she has a reservation in the dining room. Can you do something about that?"

"For you, Mr. W., anything."

Beth's drink was a frothy rainbow, and Sig's—"here you go, Mr. W.—one vodka martini, three ice cubes." As they drank to a happy vacation, the music slid from Broadway to Hawaiian. "Great group," said Sig. "My wife used to do a mean hula with them."

The musicians finished the set, came over, and welcomed Sig with embraces and kisses. Sig asked about their families, and then the talk switched to hotel gossip—who had been promoted, which celebrity couple had had a fight in the Raffia, the new chef Bucky had hired. "Red alert," the drummer said softly.

Beth followed his look. Coming toward them were Bruce and Carlotta, he as dashing as the latest Armani showing, she in something black and strapless. "Move it," said the singer, and the musicians rushed back to the stand.

Sig got up, shook hands with Bruce. "And here's your lovely daughter!"

"Well, I mean!" said Carlotta. "Such flattery!"

"It was just one of those things," crooned the singer.

"That's your song, Carlotta," said Sig. She nodded complacently, put her arms out to Bruce, and they moved onto the dance floor, gliding and dipping so elegantly the other dancers stopped to watch the performance.

"You're quite a celebrity here," Beth told Sig.

"Oh . . . well . . . Marie and I have been coming to the Royal a long time."

"Marie is your wife?"

He nodded. "She died two years ago. She—you make me think of her. She was full of pep, like you. Pretty quiet since she's gone." He looked so downhearted that Beth, feeling she had to change the subject, asked him what he did.

"Not much. I'm a lawyer, but last year I reached a Certain Age and my firm's unofficial retirement policy kicked in. They put me out to graze."

Damn, thought Beth, looking at his gloomy face, I shouldn't have asked, but as long as she had gone this far—"I'm anti-retirement," she said, and Sig said, was she indeed?

"Definitely. Bad for the health."

"Not to worry. They still give me an office, and I still have a few old clients." He grinned. "Do you know how much a lawyer charges to answer two questions?"

"How much?" she responded, going along with his change in mood.

"Five hundred dollars. You have one more question."

"Tails!" The shout, followed by laughter, came from across the terrace. At the reunion table Twinky, looking triumphant, was pocketing a coin.

"A character, that Twinky," said Sig.

"That's what his wife says, but I don't think she much likes his antics."

"Maybe they don't suit the dignity of a prominent physician."

"You mean she really is a doctor?" Beth's image of Doc presiding over benefit night faded away. "I thought Doc was a nickname," she said, mentally moving her from a ballroom to an examining room.

"Doctor Winifred Delorio is one of California's outstanding internists—if making a magazine list means anything."

"And Twinky—what does he do?" half expecting to hear that he was a professor of philosophy.

"He does all right. Remember the O'Connor's ad campaign a few years back? The one with Teddy Roosevelt—?"

"And his Rough Riders? That's Twinky's?"

" 'Bully Meal! Square Deal!' "

" 'Charge! On to O'Connor's!' " they finished together.

"Those lines are part of the language now," said Beth.

"Yep—he took a Claudia Award for that one."

"A Claudia? Nice going, Twinky."

The Raffia was one of the most perfect rooms she had ever seen. On two levels, the upper tier curving over the lower like a stage, it made her think of a movie nightclub. She could imagine Ginger and Fred dancing up the low steps, seating themselves at a candle-lit table, where everything, even the napkins, folded like fans, was in orchid tones. It was a setting for romance and repartee, for Bogie and Bacall, for Cary Grant and almost anyone.

On the lower level, at a small corner table, sat Link, looking rather silly with a lei around his neck. Sig started to speak to the captain, then, seeing Link, he said they should ask Beth's partner to join them, and without waiting for her to agree or disagree, he moved jauntily down the steps.

"Lucky you—sure I won't interfere with your date?" she heard Link say. He flung off the lei, saying he had been told he had to wear it his first night, and jumped up.

The captain guided them to an upper-tier table that commanded a view of the entire room. The tall windows had been slid open to the gentle breeze, and Beth could see out into the moonlight.

CHAPTER
10

". . . died Friday, apparently of carbon monoxide poisoning
. . . after a report linking him with a prostitute was published . . ."

Linked with a prostitute. If that was worth printing, what else
did newspapers consider . . . ? Eleanor threw the paper on the
floor. Slowly she got off the bed.

On the lanai she stood several minutes staring down at the dark
beach. Garage . . . carbon monoxide . . . smelly . . . complicated . . . uncertain. Jumping—that's different. But not if there's
sand.

Abruptly she turned and went inside. She pulled open desk
drawers, found the hotel folder, removed a brochure and read
intently.

She took a shower, dried her hair, brushing it sleek around her face. Carefully she drew in eyeliner. No lipstick, she decided.

She yanked aside dress after dress. Yes—that one.

"Do you mind if I ask where you got it?"

The happy group in the elevator had stopped talking. One of the women was staring at Eleanor.

"Oh . . . you were talking to me?"

"Your dress—I love it. It *must* be a name."

"A name?"

"Yes, who's the designer?"

"You . . . are . . . looking at the designer."

"You—that's yours?"

"I promise you—it is my design."

"Well, it's just beautiful—a dream dress. Where can I . . . ? Where do you . . . ?"

The elevator stopped at the promenade level. "Come on, Mary."

Eleanor stepped back inside.

"Forget something?"

"I forgot—to go up."

"Dream dress, dream dress," the woman called as the doors closed.

"Wish they'd hurry," said the lobby hostess.

"That L.A. flight is always late," said the night clerk. "Meeting your new boyfriend?"

"I might be." She stroked her hair, smoothed the narrow skirt of her long, flowered dress.

"His family is really stashed," said the clerk. "Did you see that rock his mother was—" The reception phone rang and he picked it up. "Gatehouse," he told the girl. "The limo's coming in."

She ran to get the leis from the cooler.

* * *

One floor below the lobby, a customer lingered in the gift shop. "I just have to have these," she said, adding banana earrings to the pile on the counter. "That does it—oh, wait." She rushed to the paperbacks, pulled out half a dozen, and threw them on the counter. "Can someone take all this up to the room?"

"Of course. Don't you want your receipt?"

"That's all right." She dashed out.

Ginny separated T-shirts, lotions, jewelry, and started punching the register.

Outside the gift shop, the macaw maneuvered upside down on its perch.

"Hello, birdie, birdie," a touristy couple said tentatively. The macaw gave a vicious squawk. They leaped back.

"Just saying 'aloha,'" said the caretaker.

"Sounded more like 'drop dead,'" said the husband. "Say, have you taught this guy any swear words?"

Eleanor left the elevator and went up the stairs to the observation deck. Languorously she paced to the very end. Far away—clusters of hotel lights dotting the coastline. The other way—the dark form of the mountain. She went back, closer to the deck's center, and lingered there, looking down at the deserted pool. From up high it seemed inches away from the cocktail terrace, where waitresses moved rapidly between tables.

With halting steps she went to the center, where two huge palm trees shot up into the night sky. The lobby looked like an architectural layout, everything pancaked—the furniture, the statues. At the entrance, between the flattened bronzes—were they Buddhas?—arriving guests trailed in, crossing the tile in slow, jet-lagged motion.

The tile—deep blue—looked like the bottom of the ocean. When she bent to look at it, she felt pleasantly giddy.

She bent farther. In the courtyard outside the shop—the macaw on its brass perch. People watching it—standing on the stone floor. Stone—that's better. That's good.

She put her hand on the rail—teak, so smooth. She looked at the palm trees—bent by years and years of wind. You could touch the fronds—if you reached way, way out.

Arms loaded with leis, the sprightly hostess stepped forward, smiling at the guest.

He smiled back, lowering his head obediently, as she held up the lei.

"Welcome to the—" Something—some peripheral movement—made her freeze. Her arms still around his neck, she saw the guest's eyes widen—his mouth open to . . .

"Oh come on," said his wife. "Imagine what they'd have to do."

He chuckled. "Yeah, standing in the courtyard shouting obscenities at a parrot." They sauntered off.

"Well, beddy-byes for you, darling," said the caretaker, thinking how much he hated the bird. "Get in that cage."

"Wow—look at this, Julio." Ginny ran out of the shop, waving a long register tape. "Do you know how much that woman spent?"

Ginny was coming toward him, waving the tape. . . . An ear-splitting shriek from above—the macaw squawked furiously. . . . Something—in front of Ginny—falling . . . horrible.

Ginny screamed.

CHAPTER
11

"I've tried and tried, but I can't think of anything good about getting old." Sig looked rather enviously at a remote table where a group of children on their own were blowing bubbles through their straws, and generally having an abandoned time. "What I especially hate is not being as sharp as I used to be."

"Rubbish!" said Beth. "Smart people—and you're smart—keep on being smart."

"In rats—" Link began.

"Even at my age?" said Sig. "I'm—"

"Don't tell!" said Beth. "It doesn't matter. I promise you, Sig, smart people keep on being smart."

"Or smarter," said Link. "In rats—"

"If age doesn't matter," said Sig, "why do I keep forgetting things?"

"Everyone forgets. Some of my students can't remember what courses they're taking."

"Studies with rats—"

"You're still on rats?"

"Showed the brain," Link continued, "actually improves with age, if it's exercised. Sort of a 'use it or lose it' theory."

"Enough." Sig held up his drink in a gesture of dismissal. "I want to know how you get to be so successful that you're in full-page ads for swanky watches. Where do you get your ideas?"

"Places like this, for one," said Link. "The people give me ideas for new wrinkles in rich."

"They've always seemed like run-of-the-mill rich to me."

"They probably are," said Link. "So I exaggerate. They have two houses—I give them four. They spend a hundred dollars on a haircut—I put them on the Concorde and fly them to Bruno Dessange in Paris."

"Sex?" said Sig. "Do you exaggerate that too?"

"You bet. From two people in a bedroom, I go to five in a—"

The waiter rolled up a table with the ingredients for their Caesar salads. They watched him rub the bowl with garlic.

"Five?" Sig looked impressed. "I'll have to read your books."

"How about plots?" Beth asked.

"Oh, plots. I steal."

"You steal?" Ever alert to plagiarism, Beth tore in, some of her colleagues would have said, like a pit bull. "From whom?"

"Only the greats."

"For example?"

"For example—a beautiful, wealthy young lady of refinement marries a much older, dried-up man."

"See?" said Sig. "Older, dried-up."

"He wouldn't be so dried-up if she weren't hell-bent on giving him a hand with his research. But he doesn't want her help. He stifles her, dominates her. And then she finds out his work is garbage. She's crushed, completely down in the dumps. Meanwhile, she meets a relative of her husband—a relative by marriage —a real hunk, brainy too—"

"Wait!" said Beth. "That's *Middlemarch*! How can you get away with copying *Middlemarch*?"

"Ah, but it's *Middlemarch* in the twentieth century. Dorothea becomes Kimberly, a successful photographer. The Reverend Casaubon becomes Jeremy Cunningham, Ph.D., an environmental researcher. The English village becomes New York."

"Environmental research. New York." She laughed. "That seems less idea-stealing than . . . Strange—I brought *Middlemarch* with me."

"I know. I saw it in your bag this afternoon. You're down on idea-stealing, aren't you? Try some of my opakapaka?"

"Certainly I am. . . . Um, good. Aren't you?"

"You bet. More?"

The three joked their way through dinner, Sig filling them in with inside information about the hotel.

There was a lull in conversation, the dining room momentarily quiet. Beth listened to distant strains of Hawaiian music and looked out at the peaceful bay. "It's so serene here," she said. "No television," she remembered. "How wise they were not to have it."

"There are things," Sig said knowingly, "that aren't in the guidebooks."

And what, they asked, did that mean?

"They don't have television because the sound would carry." The hotel, he said, had no solid doors—only shutters—and everyone, except for idiots who preferred air-conditioning, kept the slats open to get a cross-breeze. He mentioned a recently-divorced couple. "What was their name? See," Sig said proudly, "I can't remember. Anyway, by pure coincidence they both showed up the same week, each with a new partner. Hot ziggety! The battles carried through the doors and right out over the lawn."

"That's not the only way sound carries," said Beth. "On the lanai this morning, I overheard an interesting conversation." They looked at her expectantly. She hesitated, suddenly feeling as if she were betraying a confidence. "Oh, just someone on the phone. Voices do carry," she said lamely, "from lanai to lanai."

"For chrissake, Twinky! That's a six hundred dollar wine!"

"Or from table to table," Link murmured, looking over at the reunion group.

"Don't be a sore loser, Bru. Put it on Mr. Howard's bill." Twinky looked like a gleeful schoolboy.

"I can't wait to taste that wine," said Bruce. He sipped. A peculiar look crossed his face.

Twinky exploded, pounding the table. "It's apple juice!" Suzy giggled, Burt snickered, Doc chuckled but looked uneasily at Carlotta, whose lips were stretched in a pained smile.

"Mr. Platinum loses again," said Sig.

"Mr. Platinum?" said Beth.

"The staff call them the Platinum Couple." They asked why and he told them that for the Howards everything always had to be the best. "Nothing," said Sig, "is too good for the winners of the Illinois lotto grand prize."

"I don't believe it! They're lotto winners?" Beth looked at Bruce and Carlotta, so sleek, so self-assured, they could have been a *Town & Country* photograph captioned OLD MONEY. "I would have thought they'd always had the best."

"They like to give that impression."

"What did they do—before?" asked Link.

"He was an accountant. She was a receptionist, I think—something like that. It must be ten, eleven years ago that they won. I heard he bought the ticket on impulse at O'Hare—said he had a special system."

"If he had a system," said Beth, "why did he buy it on impulse?"

Sig said he hadn't thought about that.

"What was his system?" said Link. "Like the farmer who numbered the cows and bet on the numbers that gave milk first?"

Sig chuckled. "Cows! No, something with computers, I think. Whatever. I never saw anyone enjoy money more. They aren't like some winners you read about—you know, 'we'll go on a cruise, buy a mink, maybe—but I'm not moving out of my trailer.' It was a big prize, not as big as they are now, but big enough. He made some shrewd investments, and parlayed . . ."

Sig paused as the group trailed past. Twinky was joking with Bruce, saying that Doc always called him in on consultations. "I usually concur." Doc was laughing, telling him to cut it out, someone might believe him. They waved as they went by. Suzy stopped to tell them that a famous rock singer was in the room. "See, over there—I'm going to get her autograph." Then Burt said no, she couldn't do that, it would be like . . . like putting her finger in someone else's pie. They left, Suzy protesting loudly.

The breeze picked up. The waiter came over and blocked the flickering candle with a menu. Beth looked at the swaying branches and thought how protected she felt, how cared for. "I love it here. I love the feeling of being cut off from the rest of the world."

"We are pretty much cut off," said Sig. "Get past the grounds and there's nothing but lava rock—nothing closer than the next hotel, and that's miles away. I think that's why people open up to each other here. They're birds in passage, isolated, here for a limited time—so they talk freely."

"Like being on an ocean liner," said Link, "and telling a stranger your life story."

Beth sat quietly, so friendly, a friendly threesome, should read one of Link's books, can guess what they're like. She felt pleasantly tired, everything slightly out of focus. Must be jet lag, she thought, looking over at the children's table. She smiled to herself —one little girl asleep, a small boy eating petits fours from the tray. She blinked. Outside the window—that head of neatly-parted hair. Wasn't that Bucky? He was winding his way through the crowd, running—at a dignified pace, but running—zigzagging around the strolling couples. "Serpentine!" she said, giggling, and Link and Sig looked at her strangely.

CHAPTER
12

A crowd of guests penned behind a yellow cord. Hotel security telling everyone there had been an accident. "Let the police get on with it, ladies and gentlemen. Go back to your rooms."

Beyond the cordoned area, the courtyard bright as noon. Lights glaring down on racks of postcards and tote bags—and police. Taking photos. Searching the floor. Rummaging through the plantings, ruthlessly tearing at the foliage.

At the center, his back to the crowd, stood Bucky and a police captain. With them were the girl from the gift shop, sobbing wildly, and the caretaker, looking ready to pass out. "What happened?" Bucky was asking him.

"I saw . . . someone . . . go by. Then—when she hit—I heard the change fall out of her purse."

And all the while, next to them on the flagstone—stained with dark blotches—lay a covered, twisted shape.

"It's true! They really do outline the body!"

"Come on, Suzy," said Burt. "You're hysterical."

"Pretty gruesome," said Twinky. "She's splattered all over."

"She must have been up very high," said Doc, sounding clinical, detached.

Suzy was crying. "I always meant to buy her clothes."

"Her clothes?" said Beth, with a sudden sinking feeling.

"She was a designer—Eleanor Lunette," Carlotta said, and Beth dimly heard Doc murmuring that she'd played tennis with her once, very nice, but never really got to know her, and Bruce saying that they used to see her at the courts, taking lessons from Zip.

"Everyone go up. Nothing you can do here."

Sig told Beth she looked pooped, and Link said he would see her to her room. At the door, he looked at her tear-stained face. "Did you know her?"

"I didn't . . . know her."

"But . . . ?"

"I heard her . . ."

"Heard her?" She said she would explain later. "Sure you're all right?" He touched her shoulder in a way that was very comforting, and went off to his room.

"Five bodies, Dale, five of her bodies on the showroom rack. I mean, the chutzpah was so colossal. . . . They don't call it copying, darling. . . . I'd never do it. . . . Morninghills . . . a whole boutique . . . I can't afford to ship—not without money." A light flashed in her eyes. Beth gave a small scream.

"Didn't mean to scare you." A security guard approached. "Guess you didn't hear me over the surf. You okay?" he said. "Kind of late to be walking the beach."

"I'm okay. . . . I just couldn't get—what happened—out of my mind."

"Yeah, it is pretty upsetting. Did you know her?"

Beth shook her head. She started walking again, and he fell in step with her. For a while they were silent. Then Beth said, "Did she jump—or fall—or what?"

"Too soon to say. Watch it!" They veered around an incoming wave. "They have to determine the classification."

"How do they decide if it was . . . on purpose?"

"They look for psychiatric history," he said. "You know—ask family members if there was anything of a despondent nature on the part of the victim."

They had reached the end of the beach, where the waves broke high over the rocks. "Could it have been an accident?" she asked as they turned.

"Well . . . to be honest, she was drinking pretty good. An individual can get to the point where she loses balance and falls. I heard about an instance of that—an individual walking on the railing of the fifth story, and was so intoxicated, he fell."

"So you think they'll decide—"

"I'm pretty sure they'll rule it an accident. . . . Tide's going out. It's getting late—or early. The joggers will be coming out. I'll walk you back."

At the elevator he asked if she wanted him to see her to her room. "No? Well, I'll say good night then."

She watched him stride toward the West lobby. Beyond and above him, the Buddha looked down from its commanding position atop a white-staired flight. Below was the service elevator. Its doors opened, and two men wheeled out a stretcher with a body bag. "Where are they taking her?" The voice resounded through the lobby. And the booming reply—"To Hilo."

She moved to get a better look, saw them push the cart around the side of the building, saw a van move up the service drive to meet them. As discreet as a death aboard ship, she thought. Protect the holiday. Protect the Royal's guests from life—from death.

CHAPTER
13

Suicide or accident?

Hot up here. No shade. Not like last night.

Excellent photo opportunity, the brochure had said, as indeed it was. Beth, however, was interested in the area that had been fenced off. She moved beyond it and stood at the rail. Below, the lobby was alive with action. Lines at the registration desk, at the tour desk. Clusters of guests talking, laughing. Others, carrying tennis rackets, raced down the stairs and through the courtyard, where business in the shop was proceeding as usual. Outside the shop, people flipped through postcards. In a corner, at a long table, a quilt-making class sewed scraps of bright material.

At night the scene would have been quieter, emptier. What had caught Eleanor's eye as she looked down? Did she stare at the round brass table, glinting now in the sun? Beth remembered hearing that you could be mesmerized by an object and want to jump.

Accident or suicide?

"Whew! It's hot as hell!"

A couple clattered up the stairs.

"Oh, there's someone else here. Did you come to look too?" asked a short, plump woman in a jumpsuit. *Jumpsuit.* That was funny—Beth started to laugh.

"See," said the woman, "where it's fenced off. That's where she must have . . . We were on the elevator with her," she told Beth importantly.

"What was she like?" said Beth. "Did . . . she seem . . . tense?" She choked out the words between gales of laughter.

"That's what the police asked us," said the woman. She looked at Beth sympathetically. "I get that way too—some kind of hysterical reaction. No, she wasn't the least bit upset. She looked perfectly normal."

Accident, thought Beth, desperately trying to control herself.

"Not so normal, Mary," said her husband. "She looked pie-eyed to me."

Suicide?

"But she was wearing the most beautiful dress! A dream!"

"That doesn't make her normal. Maybe she jumped because it cost so much. Maybe her husband should have jumped."

"Don't you remember, Bill? It was her own design."

"She loves clothes, this one," said Bill. "And shoes! Maybe *I* should jump, Imelda."

"Oh, shut up, Bill."

"I'll jump for sure when I get the hotel bill."

Wait till Bill gets the hotel bill. Beth clenched her teeth, fighting an outburst of giggles.

"Well, bye now," said Mary. "We're going to take a helicopter to look at the volcano. Isn't this place paradise?"

Beth looked over Link's titles and picked *By Faith Alone* off the rack. "I'll take this too," she said, adding it to yesterday's *New York Times* and today's Honolulu and Los Angeles papers.

She sat in the lobby, reading. The *Times*—must be the one Dale had been reading to Eleanor—reported the Jetty Corporation was near liquidation: ". . . crucial to the company's American stores . . . among them Morninghills, Morgan Harsh, and Slicks. With tens of millions of dollars owed to them for goods supplied for Christmas, many suppliers are not shipping . . . talk of filing for Chapter 11."

Today's Los Angeles paper reported "a sense of relief as American units of Jetty Corporation filed for bankruptcy, with suppliers getting ready to ship goods to such stores as Morninghills. . . . Under a plan expected to be approved by the bankruptcy court, suppliers would be essentially guaranteed prompt payment for all goods shipped from now on. This is crucial to the company's 180 stores in America, with the spring season about to begin."

They did file. Eleanor should have waited. *Does that mean I think it was suicide?*

She turned to the obituaries. "Eleanor Lunette, 38, FASH Award winner . . . said to be depressed about business problems. Jerry Marsdorf, sales manager for the company, said . . . great loss . . . multitalented designer . . ." She studied the fuzzy photograph. Elegant face. Clever. The Honolulu paper reported that Eleanor was on her way back from Hong Kong, and had died as a result of an accident while vacationing on the Big Island.

Accident or suicide? Should I tell the police? No. Why say anything? Why invade her privacy? What purpose would it serve to reveal what I heard? a reproving voice said, but what about the noise outside her room—the interruption? No. It couldn't have been anything important. Whether suicide or accident, Eleanor's death stemmed from business problems. Suicide probably—and nothing to do with some noise outside her room.

A Dorothy Parker poem kept running through her mind: "Guns aren't lawful;/Nooses give;/Gas smells awful;/You might as well live."

But Eleanor hadn't thought so.

He sat, looking out the window.

The bitch.

Never thought she'd do it.

She was a loner—and that was convenient.

Now I've got to take chances.

People were walking by. He watched them, his eyes on their jewelry, the rings, the watches.

First try couple one . . . then two . . . then three?

He played with the knickknacks on his desk, cheap trinkets people had given him over the years. Then he looked at the display on the shelves and grinned.

What the hell, I'll try all of them. See who comes through first.

Someone looked in the window, saw him, said hello. He smiled and waved.

CHAPTER
14

THURSDAY MORNING

On the way to the jogging trail, Beth passed the fitness room and saw, among the jungle of savage machines, a red-faced Burt, battling the StairMaster. Suzy, in a red romper outfit that made her look especially like Raggedy Ann, was on a bicycle, pedaling lethargically. She waved to Beth, then pointed her out to Burt, who managed a smile while he labored up and down.

At the trail's entrance were Carlotta and Bruce, she in a jade-green leotard, doing leg stretches, he, straining against a tree, arms outthrust as if he were praying fervently for something. Fabulous day, they grunted, as Beth passed them and made her way up the incline.

A wooden sign, capped with the Royal's rainbow, informed her that the two-mile fitness trail and exercise stations provided a good cardiovascular workout. She skipped the information about heart rates and moved onto the trail, walking fast, past plumed grasses and scrubby kiawe trees where small birds, like miniature cardinals, were playing tag. Carlotta and Bruce jogged past. She watched until they vanished around a bend.

Reaching the bend, she turned, and suddenly the sun glared into her eyes. She shaded her face, saw a family of four striding toward her. Passing them in a half-jog . . . was it?—Yes, Bucky, in a white suit, looking serene, as if the event of the night before had never occurred.

Conscientiously pumping her arms, she followed the broad path as it wound through the golf course. A security truck idled by and moved onto a fairway, the driver stopping to talk to a groundskeeper. At the quarter-mile mark she picked up the pace, and nearly collided with a golf cart barreling across the trail.

When she reached the half-mile marker, she was feeling the heat, thinking she would come out earlier next time. She pushed on, looking at the cloud-covered mountain ahead—and saw Link running down a rise. "I like your Midwestern T-shirt, Professor," he said. His blue eyes gazed at her in a way that made her say matter-of-factly, "You're out early."

"Catch you on my next round," he said, and sprinted away. All at once she felt very cheerful.

Farther along, the landscape contrasted sharply with the hotel grounds. Twisted dead trees, weathered bones of branches overgrown with wild vines—it was like the beginning of *Rebecca,* she thought, when you see Manderley after the fire. She slowed. A fence, and behind it, piles of sand and big construction trucks. DANGER. DO NOT GO BEYOND THIS POINT. The trail appeared to have come to an abrupt end.

Then she saw the arrow pointing left and realized the trail had taken a sharp turn upward. She could see the entire hill, the trail circling it neatly in a series of U-bends, so that the runners ahead kept disappearing only to reappear unexpectedly, one level higher, like players in a French farce.

So hot, she thought, not like walking on the level at home. She struggled around the next bend, and there was Doc, trim in a T-shirt and black bicycle shorts, at an exercise station, doing step-ups. Beth stopped gratefully. "Where's Twinky?"

"Right here," he said, popping out of the scrub. "Found two golf balls—"

"Hawking golf balls?" said another voice. It was Zip, racing down the hill. "Is that the old aloha spirit?"

"You're late today, Zippo."

Zip smiled at Beth. "Everyone's late."

Yes, she thought, but no one's talking about why. Were they thinking about Eleanor too?

"Gotta go—have a lesson," said Zip, and he loped off, big and powerful.

At the top of the hill, next to the mile marker, thank God, a watercooler. She took several drinks from a paper cup and gazed at the hotel, so far in the distance it seemed as if she had come more than a mile. Closer, she could see Doc and Twinky winding in and out, and Zip several bends ahead of them. Sweat poured down her legs, trickling into her shoes, red with dust from the trail. She took another drink and started back.

At the halfway point, Link jogged up to meet her. "I'll go back with you," he said, turning.

"Bought one of your books," she said, walking fast.

"Which one?" He did a half-jog beside her.

"By Faith Alone."

"Enjoying it?"

"I'm sure I will"—she was sure she would not—"but first I have to finish rereading *Middlemarch.*"

"How's old Dorothea doing?"

"Not too well—she's learning what married life is like."

"Has she met Ladislaw yet?"

"Oh, long ago."

"*He'll* make her happy." Somehow he gave the comment a personal meaning.

Coming off the trail, they met Suzy and Burt. "Let's get moving," Burt was saying, then, seeing Beth and Link, he asked if they were on for tennis that afternoon.

"Okay by you?" said Link.

"Fine," she said, her mind on a couple just starting a run, so obviously a first-day pair—pale, no tan, a serious-about-exercise, guilty-about-big-breakfast look. Just checked in, probably, and untouched by Eleanor, probably didn't even know.

"See you on the courts," said Burt. "Come on, Sooze." She groaned and followed him up the path.

"Want to go for a swim?" said Link.

She looked at the green, green grass, at the beach dotted with bright umbrellas, at the swimmers surfing the waves. "I'd love to."

"Meet you back here in fifteen minutes."

She raced to her room to change, saw waitresses carrying trays of champagne and fruit to the rooms. She was in a champagne mood. From here on, her holiday was going to be perfect, and she was going to put Eleanor out of her mind.

CHAPTER
15

FRIDAY

"He's the star partner now—chairman of his law firm"—
Suzy yelling over the blow-dryer to the girl brushing her Raggedy
Ann hair into ringlets.

"He was just made CEO"—Carlotta, in a loud under-the-dryer
voice to the manicurist. "What? They manufacture computer
chips. . . . What? He has a doctorate from CalTech."

"I didn't know that about Bruce—very impressive," Beth com-
mented to Doc. They were in the salon waiting room, sitting on
soft peach sofas, sandaled feet resting on thick peach carpet, the
unwindowed womblike decor, very different from the airy, open
feeling elsewhere in the Royal.

"Impressive," said Doc, "but untrue." Then, as if regretting her disclosure, "Needs conditioner," she said, running a hand through her long hair. "The sun is really hell"—making clear she did not intend to pursue either Bruce's education or his present occupation.

"And the humidity," said Beth, accepting Doc's reticence, wondering why she had told her at all.

"Travel, dinners, speeches . . ." Suzy lifted her voice. "Oh, the speeches! Taxes this! Taxes that! So many pressures," she said, while the hairdresser held the dryer to her head like a gun. "I have to make sure he gets enough exercise, enough rest, the right things to eat." Beth listened, thinking Burt probably did an excellent job of making sure Suzy did—or accepted—all these things.

"I lay out everything in my dressing room"—Carlotta again. "What? Oh, I always get all new outfits for the Royal—every single year—new everything, down to the shoes, even"—naughty tone—"new nightgowns. More fun that way, don't you think?"

The manicurist agreed oh, yes, it must be fun—looking forward, Beth imagined, to the after-hours discussion she would hold with her coworkers. Carlotta, oblivious, went on describing this year's wardrobe, until the manicurist held up a bottle of polish and they went into a huddle about colors.

Reflecting that this was not the first time she had felt like an eavesdropper at the Royal, Beth asked Doc if she was enjoying her stay.

"Oh, always, Beth." Her voice was soft, musical. "The Royal is so much our second home that we hate to leave—Twinky made up a lovely thought. When we board the plane at Kona, he says, the Royal ceases to exist, and it doesn't come to life again until we're on the plane for Hawaii."

"That is lovely."

"Twinky is *very* creative," Doc said firmly, as if daring anyone to argue the point. "But he's under so much pressure now. He has an important campaign coming up, very high-profile account. He has to find a different slant and have it ready to present to the client when we get back."

"That can't be too big a problem for someone who could come up with the O'Connor's commercial."

"Sig told you about that," said Doc.

But why did she look so troubled? Was she afraid Twinky could no longer meet the standard he had set? "I'm sure," said Beth, "Twinky will find that new slant."

"Oh, I'm not worried." But she did look worried. "I just wish he'd get down to it. Of course, it's hard here, with all the activities and the people, and . . ." She trailed off.

And the silliness and the pranks that make you miserable, Beth silently finished the sentence.

For a few minutes they sat quietly, while salon talk swirled around them—"richest man in the world, worth seven billion . . . booked an extra room just for their luggage . . . They call him 'The Monsoon' . . . every time he's on the Island . . . Estrogens? . . . My new gynecologist—a woman, but I'm just delighted with her . . ."

Doc chuckled at the last remark, and Beth asked if she had found it difficult to get patients to accept a woman doctor.

"In the beginning, when I first went into practice, I used my initials—but that's all changed now. Women especially like to go to women. It's just amazing—*amazing*," she said, "what some women tell me about problems they've had for years and were too embarrassed to tell a male doctor."

Beth looked at Doc's reflection in the opposite mirror—features too strong for pretty; handsome rather—a face that promised reliability and sympathetic understanding. "I should think you would be a good person for anyone to talk problems over with, woman or man."

"Oh"—deprecatingly—"just being a doctor gets people to confide in you. . . . But it's important to understand a patient's personal problems if you're going to—"

"Do you ever tell Twinky?"—Suzy, emerging from the blow-dry.

"Just sit there, Mrs. Breneman. I'll get your pedicure set up."

"Tell Twinky what?" asked Carlotta, getting up from the dryer.

"Watch your nails, Mrs. Howard!"

Doc didn't answer. She was standing now, looking intently at a display of headbands.

"Tell Twinky what?" Carlotta repeated.

"Oh, Suzy just wanted to know if I tell Twinky about my patients. Think this would work for me?" She pulled a headband over her hair.

"Well, do you?" said Carlotta. "He's always saying that Doc agrees with his diagnoses."

Beth waited, resenting the question on Doc's behalf. No wonder she didn't want to dignify it with an answer. "Of course she doesn't," she said indignantly when Doc failed to reply. "That would be breaking doctor-patient confidentiality."

Doc removed the headband. "Twinky likes to joke," she said coolly, "but no, I do not tell him about my patients," and Beth admired her for keeping her temper.

There were shouts of "ooh, what's this?" as the shampoo girl came in with a tray. "Donetta's birthday. Have some cake."

"Let's really celebrate," said Carlotta, "and have drinks. Come on everyone—they're on me," and a call was put in to the bar, the girl telling them to hurry, she had a facial coming in.

"Aren't you having any cake?" someone asked Doc, in a booth now, where the girl was winding her thick hair around huge rollers.

"Think I'll pass."

"That's discipline," said Carlotta, watching the mirror closely as the girl teased her hair into its grand sweep.

"And Doc knows how to use *all* the machines in the fitness room," said Suzy. "Burt would love it if I could do that—Burt would love it if I had her figure."

Figure was a cue word. The subject surged up and down the line of booths, expanding, as the talk flowed, like cellulite—"biggest behind I ever saw . . . desperate to get my thighs down . . . frantic to lose ten pounds before the wedding . . . Diamond Doorways—they taught me how to eat nine hundred *good* calories a day . . . had her eyes done . . . fifty, looked like thirty . . . just like Grace Van Owen . . . you know, *L.A. Law* . . ."

"Oh, that's good." Suzy sighed as the manicurist massaged lotion into a chubby leg. "Just what I needed." She sounded very low.

"Why so sad, Suzy?"

"I don't know. Yes, I do—I was thinking about *L.A. Law.* I know it sounds silly, but before we came, I was up late, watching a rerun from two, three years ago . . . whatever . . ." She shook the suds off the other foot. "It got to me."

What got to her?

"Everything—everyone. Mickey, just starting out, ready to save the world. Grace, bouncy, in love. Stewart still a bachelor, looking so carefree. I mean, they looked so young," Suzy said wistfully, "and it made me feel so *old.* And then I started thinking how fast things change, and how I wouldn't even have noticed if it hadn't been a rerun, and then"—she struggled to express her thought—"and then I started thinking we're changing, too, and we don't even notice, and when we do notice it's too late to do anything." She giggled as the girl ran the emery over the sole of her foot. "That tickles."

One of the shampoo girls told Beth she was sorry, they were running late, and she would be with her in a minute. That was all right, Beth said, her mind on Suzy, wondering what she had meant. Too late to do anything about what? Not getting older, surely.

"Suicide or accident?" The conversation had turned to Eleanor Lunette, and the entire salon was taking part, the discussion swaying back and forth. "What do you think, Beth?" said Carlotta. "We need a professor's opinion."

Oooh, a professor, the girls said, as everyone turned away from the mirrors. The whole salon seemed to be looking at her, awaiting her judgment.

"I think . . ." She paused. She did not want to say suicide, because then she would have to explain why.

"I'm here for a facial." Saved, by the man in a *yukata* who had just come in the door. "Got a lot of sun," he said. The girl told him the treatment was just perfect for that and she led him off to the back regions of the salon.

"So, Beth, what do you think?" said Carlotta.

"Oh . . . accident."

"You sound doubtful—do you really mean it?"

"Ready now, Miss—Professor—Austin." Saved again. She followed the girl into the shampoo room.

CHAPTER
16

For a few days, life at the Royal was all a holiday should be. Beth fell into a routine of mornings on the trail followed by the beach with Link, afternoon tennis with the reunion group, and evenings with Sig and Link. Then came a three-day period of tension that Beth later said should have been called the Ides of February.

MONDAY EVENING

From the beginning, Carlotta was on the warpath. "Look at the empty tables! And they made us wait until eight-thirty. Bad enough we have to be in Second City."

Second City was the main dining room, a slick, stretch limo of a room, shiny dark woods, polished black floor, one long side all windows, open to the ocean and the stars.

The waiter had hardly started to recite the evening's specials, when Bruce interrupted. "Why wasn't my drink on the table?"

"In the Raffia," said Carlotta, "our drinks are always waiting for us. . . . Totally unacceptable. Look at those zombies!" She gestured toward a far table, where the Cutora dealers were chugalugging drinks. Just then a man stood and wiggled his hips in a hula. "My God—he's barefoot!"

"Not barefoot," said Twinky. "Just loafers without socks—all the rage at the best country clubs. You should know that, Carlotta."

She and Bruce gave him a look, while Doc rapidly nibbled up the crudités in the crystal bowl.

Two waiters placed the orders on the table and ceremoniously, in one well-timed movement, held the four silver covers aloft.

Bruce stared at his plate as if it were crawling with scorpions. "What is this?"

"Your poached salmon, sir."

"This is the way you're making poached salmon?"

"It's a new presentation, sir."

"Totally unacceptable," said Carlotta.

Bruce snapped his fingers. "Where's the second wine?" He held up an empty bottle.

"Sorry, sir. We're very rushed tonight."

"Rushed!" He threw the bottle at the waiter, who just managed to catch it.

"That's not the old aloha spirit," said Twinky.

Coffee arrived for the second time, Carlotta having rejected the first service as cold. "Did you notice," she said, "the way he *throws* the cup on the saucer?"

Doc said they were short-staffed because of the luau, and they should have gone with Suzy and Burt. Carlotta said it wasn't the luau, they were giving all the service to that bunch of hicks. Groups, said Bruce, did not take suites, and for what they were paying, the Royal could hire more staff. Totally unacceptable, said Carlotta, and Bruce should talk to Bucky.

"I just made up a poem," said Twinky. "Want to hear it?" They glared at him. "Ah, I see you do. The title," he announced, "is 'Totally Acceptable.'" Solemnly he cleared his throat and began to recite.

> *It's okay*
> *In every way*
> *For New Money*
> *To act funny.*

And what was that supposed to mean, said Carlotta and Bruce. "Nothing at all. Twinky is in one of his moods," said Doc, her hand moving toward the silver tray of petits fours. Systematically, she began eating macadamia nut cookies.

The waiter came with a folder, their bill inside. Bruce took out a fifty. "See that," he said. "That's your tip." He struck a match, lit a corner of the fifty, and let it burn to ashes.

"Pow! What an ending," said Link. He and Sig and Beth had been watching the drama from a nearby table.

"The magic isn't working," said Sig, fingering a shiny leaf on the tablecloth. "The ti leaf is for harmony at the table."

"Harmony! I thought the waiter was going to kill Bruce—he should have," said Beth. "And what's the matter with Twinky? Wasn't his humor rather forced tonight?"

"I'd say insolent," said Link. He took out a notebook. "Great plot potential."

TUESDAY AFTERNOON

Almost a formal pattern, Beth thought. Lots of perpendiculars—tall palm trunks, upright umbrellas, bare straight backs of people standing, sharp right angles of people sitting. And a symmetry in their viewpoint—the lifeguard looking out at the waves through binoculars, the guests staring at the ocean—everyone facing the water. Like a tropical Grande Jatte.

"No embraces! Pick up the paces! Kick sand! in their faces!" The cheer came from the grassy spot toward the end of the bay, where Beach Olympics—the reunion group against the tennis pros—had been going on all afternoon. Tug-of-war, coconut toss —the weird games had drawn a crowd.

All morning and all night, apparently, Twinky had been running around organizing the event, making up cheers, then badgering the staff into photocopying them so they could be memorized, trying to get special T-shirts printed, settling for yellow shirts and red wigs. Where he had found the red wigs for his team was a mystery, but it was a good way, Beth thought, to put off working on the new campaign.

Now Suzy, Carlotta, and Doc were shaking pom-poms and chanting—*"Pineapples, papayas, lilikoi juice! What have you got? Hawaiian Fruits!"* The tennis pros groaned and came back with a cheer of their own. Beth couldn't catch all the words, something about being built like sequoias—and as old.

Volleyball—the final event—was starting. Beth watched the ball go back and forth and listened to the jibes. Burt seemed to be enjoying himself most of all. "Kill, kill, kill! Don't take any prisoners!" He jumped for the ball and missed. Strange; he was well built, muscled, but his movements were awkward. No matter how much he worked out or how many lessons he took, Burt would never be an athlete. Suzy made a good hit—Zip killed it with a powerful return.

Beth opened *Middlemarch*. For a while she was absorbed, drawn into the story. Then her surroundings proved too enticing. She closed the book and stared at the water, studying the changing shadows and colors. She listened to the waves, entranced by the sound pattern, sometimes louder, muting the laughing voices—sometimes   softer—louder . . . softer . . . louder . . . softer. She closed her eyes.

"Let's give everyone a hand!" That was Zip's voice. Beth looked around dizzily, feeling disoriented. Empty chairs where there had been people. People in chairs that had been empty. "Let's hear it for both teams!" Cheers. Applause. The teams were headed her way.

Then a man in a suit ran up to Burt. "Mr. Breneman?"

Burt nodded, sweaty, looking slightly ridiculous in the red wig.

"I'm from the *Honolulu Advertiser*. We're doing a series on tax law—and when we heard you were here, we thought, what a break! Could you give us an interview?"

Burt looked pleased. "I feel a little silly," he said. "Do I have time to change?"

"Sir, we'd like to—but we have a deadline."

"Oh, fire away."

"That's great! Just give us a minute to set up." He motioned to his crew. Chairs were moved back and forth, and so was Burt: in front of a palm—"No, the light's wrong"; under another palm—"No, that's no good, you can see the bar in the background."

Finally the camera rolled. The interviewer threw questions, and Burt, stiff and prim, answered pompously, with frequent pedantic digressions. Suzy stood to one side, looking proud. The others stretched out on the grass.

After fifteen minutes or so, the man thanked Burt and handed him a card. Burt read it, and frowned.

What was on the card, Burt? everyone asked. What did it say?

"Twinky Delorio Television Productions," Burt said in a small voice.

Twinky roared, rolling over and over on the grass. "I hired them! You looked so serious, Burt, sitting there in your wig, talking about capital gains."

Burt felt for the wig, mumbling that he had forgotten to take it off. He was sweating profusely now and red dye from the wig ran down his face.

"Twinky." Suzy sounded miserable. "I'm not sure that was really funny."

"All in good fun," said Burt. "Stop crying, Suzy."

Beth looked around for Doc, spotted her at the beach bar scarfing down Maui chips.

WEDNESDAY MORNING

Too late. He reached the ball too late and sent it into the net.

"He should have known they'd hit to his backhand volley," Zip told Beth. They were on the terrace, watching a men's doubles match. Zip got up. "Aloha! You're late."

The group shambled onto the terrace, dragging themselves along. Zip gave his booming laugh. "You look like you're going to your own executions!"

He was right, Beth thought. They looked terrible, especially Bruce. Pale, unshaven, he made her think of freshman boys who started a beard before midterms, when everyone's nerves were frazzled. "Let's get started," he said grimly, and he and Carlotta walked off with Twinky and Doc.

Beth missed Link, who was on the beach finishing his writing stint for the day. But Zip was a good partner, keeping the ball in play when he could have put it away, shouting encouragement to everyone.

Burt hit a winner down the alley.

"Well done, Tax Expert," Zip called, patting a hand against his racket, and Beth wondered again who it was that Zip reminded her of. No matter. But she wished he had not made a remark that inevitably would remind Burt of yesterday's humiliation.

Sure enough, from that point on, Burt's game fell apart. The worst was when he swung with brute force to put away an easy smash—he missed completely, and hit himself in the head. It was hard not to laugh, and Zip didn't even try. "Too much breakfast," he boomed. "All those calories are making the tax expert a tiger."

Suzy was no help, stopping in the middle of a point to get a drink, repeatedly asking the score, and positively obsessing about the balls. "Where's the third one?" she called, as Zip started to serve.

Burt slammed his racket to the ground. "We have three balls! *He* has all three because he is serving. *Can you understand that?*"

"Yes, I can—you don't need to yell." And she hit the next return so angrily, she put it away. She looked thinner, Beth thought. You could almost see her cheekbones. Maybe Burt's fitness routine was working.

The round was a disaster, over quickly. "You'll do better next time," Zip said jovially, slapping Burt on the back.

They sat in the shade and watched the other foursome.

Twinky was playing as usual, joking, clowning. Then he hit a powerful winning forehand. "Charge, men!" Zip called from the sidelines. "Just like T.R.!" Twinky looked as if he had just been told about a death in the family.

From that moment, Twinky's game disintegrated as rapidly as Burt's. Once he ran forward from the back court to hit a shot Doc had missed, slipped and slid into the net. Everyone waited for him to yell at Doc. "Oh shit," he said. "I *knew* I was going to do that."

"My God," said Carlotta, "that's the first time he's ever admitted it was his own fault, and Doc doesn't look happy. Doc—you should be thrilled he's finally taking the blame."

A few points later Bruce swung and missed. "That was mine," Carlotta yelled. "Stop poaching!"

"Be nice, Bru," Zip called. "Share with your friends."

"Share what?" Bruce sounded jittery.

"The glory, of course," said Zip. But why, Beth wondered, did Zip look so pleased with himself?

Now it was Bruce's turn to fall apart. He hit any old way, making no effort to control his shots. Twinky yelled at him not to serve so hard to Doc. Then Bruce hit Doc with a stinging forehand. "Oh, sorry," he said. "Thought you were crossing over."

"Don't worry about it." She rubbed her knee.

"You did it on purpose!" Twinky threw his racket at Bruce, jumped over the net, and punched him in the nose. In a few seconds, they were slugging it out.

"Hey," said Zip. "That's not the old aloha spirit." He ran over and pulled them apart.

The group left for their rooms, nursing wounded feelings—and wounds. Bruce looked as if he was going to have a black eye.

"My, my," said Link, who had arrived with Sig just in time for the fight. "Our fun people are certainly acting strange."

Sig nodded sagely. "Mixed doubles means mixed troubles."

"Great conflict," said Link. "Can't have a story without conflict."

Beth agreed absently. She had just remembered. Zip reminded her of an arrogant student she'd had a few years back. He had made free with her office, stopping by at all hours without an appointment. Once she had come in late and found him reading the papers on her desk.

Later Beth went to the tennis desk to check the time for tomorrow's game—if there was a game.

"The chutzpah of her—just colossal"—this from the tennis assistant as she hung up the phone.

At once something echoed in Beth's mind. "Where did you get that?"

"Oh, this woman. She's so pushy—always wants me to pair her with A players."

"No, no—I mean 'colossal chutzpah.' Where did you get that expression?"

"Oh that. Guess I picked it up from Zip."

CHAPTER
17

THURSDAY MORNING

The sprinklers and the birds had kicked in at the same time—three-fifteen—and she had never been able to get back to sleep. Beth looked at the clock—almost six. She put on a T-shirt and shorts, and left the room.

In the atrium she passed silent rooms and shuttered doors. Through the slats she could see clothes strewn over chairs, dropped casually after a late night. Down the stairs—wasn't that Suzy, in her red romper outfit, ambling down the opposite stairway? She was carrying a mug. Must be heading for the dining terrace, where coffee and rolls were set up for early risers.

Down to the promenade. A bellboy in flowered shirt and white pants walked down the corridor at an unhurried Hawaiian pace.

Past the empty pool. Past the fitness room—only Burt, pedaling away.

On the beach, in the faint early light, the working hotel had come to life—a machine smoothed the sand; a beachboy swabbed chairs; another pushed a cart of towels.

The earliest regular, Lean and Mean, arms swinging triumphantly, was just coming off the trail. He grunted in reply to Beth's good morning. He was followed by Slow Jog, who gave Beth her usual exhausted smile. Knee Bandage was missing—he must have checked out.

She went up the incline, walking fast. On the golf course a groundskeeper dragged a length of hose into a white truck. A security truck circled around him. The two exchanged waves.

She moved past the golf crossing, her thoughts on her late-night reading. So many about-to-be disillusioned couples in *Middlemarch*. So many husbands and wives who thought they had found in each other what they could never hope to find. Were there, she wondered, elements of the *Middlemarch* pairs in the reunion group? Behind the banter, she sensed strain—desperation even.

Or was she exaggerating? If, in the last few days, the jibes had become cruel, if there had been a joylessness in their eagerness to enjoy themselves, it was from overindulgence, surely—too much sun, too much food, too much exercise—like shipboard life when passengers tried to cram a year's vacation into a week's voyage.

She picked up the pace, her mind again turning to the question that had kept her wakeful. Why *colossal chutzpah*? Well, why not? The phrase was everywhere, even a book title. No, not true— chutzpah maybe, but not colossal. And was it a commonplace for a tennis assistant from Texas? Of course it was not. She had picked it up from Zip.

But was a phrase more typical of Seventh Avenue than Hawaii a commonplace for Zip? What if the Seventh Avenue phrase came to Hawaii—as it had. And what if someone else had overheard? Preposterous. Coincidence, that was all. And what did it matter? She intended to ask Zip, though, next time she saw him.

As she passed the wild Manderley scene, she glanced at her watch. When I'm home and I wake up at this time, I'll hear the wind screaming outside, and I'll remember I was just here, feeling a warm breeze.

Atop the hill, at the mile marker, she brushed the sweat off her face and took a drink. Far below, a gray-haired man appeared— Bruce?—made the turn, and raced upward toward the first bend. Then she saw the unmistakable jade leotard—Carlotta, just turning. It would take them a while to get here.

She took another drink, thinking idly that if this were a mystery, someone would have put poison in the watercooler. But how to figure out when the right victim would take a drink. She laughed at herself, tossed the cup into the wire basket, already partly full. Bruce arrived, followed soon after by Carlotta. They were at the exercise station, doing quadricep stretches, when Beth started back.

Downhill always went smoothly. So lovely with the sun coming up. Going to be a beautiful day. What would she have for breakfast? Indulge in eggs Benedict? She felt so good she had to run. She raced along, thinking that she would see how far she could get before Bruce and Carlotta passed her. A dash past the Manderley wilds—suddenly, the sun was in her eyes, blinding her. She turned her head to escape the glare, and something made her slow. A glimpse of red, deep in the scrub, like a flag commanding her to go back. Reluctantly, she turned.

Branches scratched her face as she clambered downward. She stumbled toward the bottom—almost fell—caught herself. She hadn't realized the incline plunged so deep. Things buzzed in her face—she slapped them away. She reached the branches— stopped abruptly.

She felt sick. A body, stretched out in a stillness so absolute it was almost agonizing. She knelt—no pulse. Then, knowing all the time what she would see, she made herself pull the vines off the face.

Oh Jesus Christ—and all that goes with it. This was impossible. This was a holiday. This was a bloody mess. She choked off a laugh—can't ask about chutzpah now. Too late. He had checked out. She laughed and laughed and the laugh became a scream that echoed over the trail and brought a dumbfounded look to the face of the security guard who stood looking down at her.

As the security truck roared down the hill she saw Twinky and Doc. They were in jogging clothes—sweaty, as if they had just finished a run. What was Doc staring at?

Beth looked down and saw blood splashed all over her T-shirt and shorts in gaudy streaks, like a hideous tie-dye.

"The tennis pro. Yeah. Right away." The guard spoke into the walkie-talkie.

"Was he breathing? You're sure?" asked Doc.

She heard the guard giving Doc the gruesome details, but what stood out in her mind was Twinky. "Old Zip?" His voice came out in a croak. "Someone slit his throat? That's—that's—that's not the old aloha spirit."

CHAPTER
18

Midafternoon, the same day. Beth, Sig, and Link on the open terrace next to the main dining room. Bright, bright, bright outside. The sun in the hands of a lighting director, now spotlighting the metal rackets of players headed for the courts, now the purple towels of people headed for the beach. From stage left, somewhere near the pool: "Where you going?" "Taking a massage." "Don't forget our hula lesson." So jolly, Beth thought. Would it be the same as with Eleanor in a few days, she wondered—as if Zip's death had never happened?

Nearby, in the shaded courtyard—where Eleanor's crumpled body had lain—stood two men, one so stocky he almost blocked out the other. She could hear them making plans to have lunch sometime.

"Who's that with Bucky?" said Sig.

"The chief of police," said Link. "They wouldn't even let *him* inside the barrier."

"You were out on the trail?" said Beth, seeing the blood on the branches, on the ground, on the dreadfully limp body. "Why would you go there?"

"Scene of the crime—maybe my next will be a mystery. Why fight it? Two yellow ribbons in a week—around the grounds they tie the yellow ribbons."

"Not funny," said Sig, his flowered shirt an ironic contrast to his gloomy face. "It's terrible—for the hotel, for the employees—terrible about Zip." Link said he was glad that he had included Zip. Sig grunted and slumped back in his chair.

"What did you see?" Beth asked Link.

"Police rummaging through the dirt like a bunch of book reviewers searching for symbols. They were putting things in plastic bags—stones, candy wrappers."

Sig sat up. "There couldn't have been many wrappers—not at the Royal." He slumped again, and closed his eyes.

"You're right—mostly stones. I couldn't see the body. They had it wrapped like a Christo."

"Good thing too," said Beth, thinking of the dark gaping wound under Zip's chin.

"What did he look like?"

"He looked . . . like a jack-o'-lantern."

"And it's not even Halloween," Link said lightly, as if he refused to be mournful. "What do you think it was done with?"

"I don't know. Knife? Razor?"

"A claw, maybe? Wolfman hits Hawaii. It had to have been someone very strong. Zip was a big guy."

"He could have been caught off guard," said Sig, coming out of his trance.

A Japanese couple, toting bags of souvenirs, wandered onto the terrace. They walked around, talking excitedly, gazing at the ocean, admiring the flowers. Then they came up to the table, conveying with sign language that they wanted someone to take their picture.

"I'll do it," said Link. "Pretty fancy equipment." He took the camera they held out, and posed them against the low wall, with the ocean in the background. Then he stood them in front of the bronze reflecting pool. "Make a wish—whatever you want will come true." They looked bewildered. "Never mind . . . smile— no, smile! Say Halloween!" They giggled. "That's it. . . . But how," he said, returning to the table, "could you catch someone off guard on the trail? He must have seen whoever it was."

The tennis assistant came by. Her face was mottled, as if she had been crying. Sig patted her arm and asked how she was doing.

"Why, why?" she cried out. "I told the police it doesn't make sense. Zip never hurt anyone. Everyone was crazy about him." She clenched her hand into a fist. "I hope they find that—"

"They'll find him, Gail," Sig said comfortingly. "Who are they questioning?"

"Beachboys, grounds workers, guests—everyone who was out early. I've got to get back. The mixed doubles round-robin is full up and people are screaming for court times. Can you believe it? You'd think they'd give us a break."

They watched her run down the steps to the courts. Then Link said, "So tell us, Beth, what did the detectives ask you?"

"Detective—singular. He wanted to know what I had for breakfast."

"That's the procedure," Link said knowingly. "Go back to the beginning, ask innocuous questions, catch the killer off guard."

"I had the perfect motive—he wouldn't give me the lesson time I wanted."

"What *did* you have for breakfast?"

"I didn't—I was out before breakfast."

"Then you could have seen the killer coming off the trail."

"It couldn't have been anyone coming off. There was nothing at—in the scrub when I ran past the first time. At least I think there wasn't." She suddenly remembered she hadn't really looked until the sun in her eyes had made her turn her head. With less assurance, she said, "I think it must have been just before I started the back mile—sometime after six forty-five."

"Very suspicious—she knows the exact time."

"Where were you, Link?" Sig asked. "You usually jog early."

"On my lanai, wrestling with a plot problem. And I can prove my innocence if Beth's right about the time. 'Aloha! Room Service!' That's just when she rolled in with my lox omelet."

Betty, from the cocktail terrace, appeared, her face tense, worried. "Sit down, Betty," said Sig. "Talk to us." He pulled out a chair.

"Oh, I shouldn't," she said, settling into the chair. "It's so horrible—for *that* to happen to someone in the family."

Link looked puzzled. "Zip was in your family?"

"He was in the Royal family—guests, staff, we're all like *ohana*. No one in the family could have done this. They're questioning the wrong people." They asked what she meant, and she said that her brother-in-law with the Hapuna Police had told her they had a report to be on the lookout for kids from a Honolulu boys' home. "That's who they should be looking for! They're a bad bunch; they'd do anything for money."

"But people don't usually carry money when they're jogging," Beth said gently.

"Those kids wouldn't know that. It *has* to be someone outside the hotel. Oh, it's horrible, I feel so frightened—they should call the kahuna."

"Kahuna?" said Link.

"The priest who blessed the grounds. Before they built the Royal, he walked the property from the top of the road—where the main entrance is now—to the golf course area, and he blessed all that, and then he went to the hotel area and blessed that. And then he went down and opened his arms to the bay. He said it was so beautiful to feel the sun, feel the nourishment. 'Betty,' he told me, 'in years to come they will build many hotels along the coastline, but that hotel will be special. That hotel will have guests that will return over and over, and when they leave the aloha spirit will go back with them. You must work there,' he said. 'Employees will have a very special aloha in the hotel and that's why the guests will come back over and over. You have to stand in the bay,' he told me, 'and put out your right arm.'

"And I did what he said. I was hired in June of that year, and one night when the sun was about to set I went down to the bay and I remembered he said open your right hand, and I felt the warmth. And now"—tears rolled down her cheeks—"the hotel will lose its aloha."

"It's going to be okay, Betty," said Sig. "The Royal will never lose the aloha spirit."

She shook her head. "I don't know, but thank you, Mr. W. My heart has much aloha for you." Slowly she got up. "But they should call the kahuna! The grounds must be reblessed—before something else happens. It comes in threes!" She stood there, rock solid. Cassandra in a muumuu, Beth thought, but, as Sig said, it was not funny. Before they could think of anything to say, she left them.

"Maybe it is the old loiterer solution," said Link. "If not the kids, someone else from off the property."

"I doubt it," said Beth, remembering the careful check at the entrance gate, the security trucks patrolling the beach and the trail. "The Royal is very enclosed. It wouldn't be that easy to get on and off the grounds without being seen. Sig, will you do something for me?"

"Darling, for you, anything."

"Get the phone call record on Eleanor Lunette."

"Who's that?"

"You know—the designer."

"The woman who fell? What does she have to do with anything?"

She hesitated. It was hardly the time to explain *colossal chutzpah*. "Just a feeling," she said.

"What are you up to, Beth?" said Link, giving her a curious look, a mix of admiration and anxiety.

"I'm not up to anything. It's just that . . . puzzles interest me."

"Then do another crossword. You could be putting yourself in danger."

Stop it! she wanted to say. A bright guy—but save me, O Lord, from overprotective men. "What's so risky?" she said, a deliberate edge to her voice. "It's just a phone record. . . . Please, Sig?"

"Well . . . I would, but it's not that easy."

"Sig, you can do anything you want at this hotel."

"Hey, I'm not the manager."

"Mr. Winterfield." It was the boy from the gift shop. "I have something for you."

Sig unwrapped the package. "My cigars! Super! Where'd you find them?"

"My mother picked them up in Waimea. Oh, that's all right"— refusing a bill from Sig. "No problem. Let me know if you need more."

"See what I mean?" said Beth.

LATE AFTERNOON

The quiet interval before dinner, the time for a massage, for a nap, for making love. At the front desk, the clerk threw back his head and roared. " 'There are some things even rats won't do!' That's a good one, Mr. Winterfield." They chuckled, exchanged a few more stories.

Sig lowered his voice. "Jimmy, my boy, can you do an old man a favor?"

Just before they went in to dinner, Sig took Beth aside and handed her a long sheet. "This is a printout of her bill. You'll notice it includes phone calls—numbers, times—and don't ask me how I got it!"

CHAPTER
19

My God, four A.M. She had been reading *Middlemarch* for two hours—no, not reading, turning pages. Somewhere she had heard that if you can't sleep, you should get out of bed. . . . She slid the screen open and stood on the lanai, looking at the moonlit ocean, listening to the beat of the waves. In the distance, flickering against the darkness, was a ring of lights, one blinking steadily, on, off, on, off. . . .

But what do I have to go on, she asked herself, returning for the umpteenth time to the subject that had kept her wakeful. She was only guessing that Zip had overheard the same conversation she had, guessing that between his death and Eleanor's there was some link. Link. She had a great title for his mystery—*The Colossal Chutzpah Connection.*

All right, she thought, let's say Zip *was* outside the room. Let's say he did hear Eleanor's conversation. So what? She didn't know.

And if he was outside the room, what was he doing there? The interruption, if there was one—she was becoming doubtful, even of that—was short. If Zip had been there, he hadn't come in.

She went inside, turned on all the lights, and looked over the newspaper articles about Eleanor. Then she turned to the printout of the hotel bill. Eleanor had called Room Service several times. She had made one local call—to the airline—and two calls to New York. Beth stared at the New York numbers. What time is it there? She glanced at the clock—four-thirty. Let's see, eight-thirty in Chicago, so it's nine-thirty in New York.

"Lunette Designs." The bright voice seemed at odds with the darkness outside.

"Is . . ." Beth grabbed the newspaper. "Is Jerry Marsdorf there?"

"This is Jerry." Another busy beginning-of-the-day voice.

"Oh, for chrissake," he said, after she told him it was Beth Austin calling from Hawaii. "Do I need this? I've got nothing more to tell you, *Hawaii Five-O.*" When she said she was not with the police: "If you're with the Royal, you can tell your boss I'm still thinking about suing."

"I'm not. . . . I'm a friend."

"I've never heard her mention you."

"Probably because I'm . . . Ellie's friend from the Royal." She waited for him to say no one ever calls her Ellie. He didn't. "Ellie and I—over the years—we always seemed to be here at the same time."

"Just a sec . . . Did you order the black satin buttons?" he shouted. "We're almost out." Beth imagined a harried assistant in a crowded room where a row of women bent over sewing machines. "So," said Jerry, "what can I do for you?"

"Frankly, I'm troubled about Ellie's death."

"Troubled? That's an understatement. What are you"—hostile again—"some kind of Shlock Holmes?"

"It's just that . . . I can't get Ellie out of my mind. That last day we had a long talk. She showed me her sketch of the Harlow."

"She showed you the Harlow?"

"She showed me all her sketches."

"You *must* have been friends." The gruff voice was warmer now. "Then you know she was a great gal and a fantastic designer."

"It was always so interesting to talk to Ellie. She was telling me about the stealing that goes on." Beth repeated the *colossal chutzpah* remark.

Jerry chuckled. "That's Ellie. Originality was her shtick. You know she won the FASH Award for her Silvery Screen line. After that, there were write-ups all over—'new talent,' 'new star on the horizon'—Ellie was going places. Now everything's so fouled up. I'm struggling with a new designer who's green as grass. She only knows from Ivana *shmatas*. . . . I'm going to sue that hotel. I'd fly out there and look the place over myself if I had the time," and he muttered something about a weak railing.

"Then you think it was an accident?"

"What else could it have been?"

"I don't know—she seemed worried about business."

Jerry made a scoffing noise. "You think she— Give me a break! Ellie was tough. She'd never have killed herself over business problems. She knew we'd work it out. I want to tell you something about these ritzy places!" And he exploded: "Mismanagement . . . bungling . . . hell to pay . . ."

He raged on and she listened, looking out into the darkness until he tapered off with talk of hauling the Royal into court. Then she said, "Did Ellie ever mention Zip Heinz?"

"No . . . just a sec. What's wrong with the collar? Looks okay to me. Now, who's this Hanzes?"

"Heinz—Zip Heinz—the tennis pro at the Royal."

"Don't remember—but she could have known him. She played tennis in New York, probably took lessons in Hawaii. Ellie was a perfectionist, wanted to do well at everything she tried. . . . Hang on. There is no pomegranate! There is no chive! We do have it in titanium. . . . Listen, it's nuts here."

"Just one more thing. Ellie mentioned Dale to me."

"Dale Palermo?"

"That's it. Do you know him?"

"Dale"—his voice turned cold—"is a woman. Tell your boss to call my lawyer."

All right, she'd slipped and let Jerry find her out. A little humiliation is part of life. She checked the other New York number and reached for the phone.

"Interesting Interiors."

"Is Dale Palermo there?"

"May I ask the nature of the call?" said the voice, after Beth had identified herself.

"I'm calling about her friend . . . Ellie Lunette."

A few minutes wait. Then—"Dale Palermo here"—a composed voice, cool as a lawyer. "Who is this?" Quickly Beth explained that she was not with the hotel or the police, that she was a guest. "Then you know—knew—Ellie?"

"Yes—" Beth broke off. She couldn't lie anymore, especially not to this clear probing voice. "No," she said, "I didn't, but I feel as if I did."

"I don't understand." The voice had turned to icicles.

"Please don't hang up. Let me explain. My room is—was—very near Ellie's. The day she died I was on my lanai, and I heard her talking with you. I couldn't help listening. I'm sorry, but she sounded so interesting, she seemed so excited about her designs . . ." Beth recounted the highlights of what she had heard. "And so," she ended, "it was just an overheard conversation, but there was something about it that made me feel an affinity . . . for your friend."

"What was it"—again the lawyerlike tone—"that made you feel this . . . affinity?"

"This seems silly . . . but remember when she was telling you about the designer whose work was copied? She was so irate. I'm the same way. I'm an English professor at Midwestern University."

"Midwestern—in Vinetown?" And Beth was granted a reprieve because Dale, it seemed, had a nephew, a senior at Midwestern, who was applying to law school.

They talked a few minutes about Midwestern, and the courses Beth taught. "So you see," said Beth, "I get indignant, too—about plagiarism, about any form of copying, really."

"I know what you mean. Of course, Ellie detested the copying that goes on," said Dale, her voice sympathetic and—what? Another note, almost guarded. "She was very creative—you know she won the FASH Award a few years back."

"Yes, the Silvery Screen line. At any rate, I felt this affinity—and I've been troubled by her death, as if I've lost a friend."

"I did lose a friend," said Dale. "We were friends for years—ever since Pratt."

"She was worried about business, wasn't she?"

"You're asking that because you think it wasn't an accident. But you're wrong. Ellie *was* worried. You know that if you heard the conversation. And she was on edge. But she was a very determined person, very self-confident—almost overconfident. The point is she would never have reacted that way to business problems. If—if she did jump, it had to have been for some other reason."

Silence for a few moments. Then Beth said, "Dale, was there an interruption in your conversation—or did I imagine it?"

"No, you didn't imagine it. There was something, I'm not sure what—someone at the door? But she seemed different afterward, you know, down."

"Any idea why?"

"No—maybe it was just a bad connection. Maybe she wasn't feeling down. I could have been imagining too."

"I don't think you were. Dale, did she ever mention Zip Heinz?"

"Sounds familiar . . . Oh, the tennis pro. Sure, she always took lessons from him when she made her R & R stops back from Hong Kong."

They seemed to have reached a dead end. Beth fished for ideas. "What was it like at Pratt?"

A pause. "There were the three of us, Ollie, Ellie, and me. The inseparables—OED, they called us."

"Who's Ollie?"

"Oliver Ritchie. We all worked together—I was into design then, classic sportswear, very clean lines." I bet they were clean, Beth thought, and I bet your interiors are cool, spare, and mono-chromatic. "Ellie," Dale went on, "was into a dressy look, but very sophisticated."

"What about Ollie?"

"Ollie?" Again the guarded note. "Ollie was into slink. He did after-five clothes, very theatrical, soap opera really. You know, sequins and satin for the supermarket. He did one offbeat line, decided it wasn't for him, and went back to the soaps look."

They talked some more. Beth asked if she remembered any-thing more about Zip, but Dale said nothing special, other than an impression that he was very friendly—nothing else really. Noth-ing more to be gained. Beth thanked her and Dale promised that if she had any more ideas, she would let her know.

Beth put down the phone, leaned back against the pillows, and sat quietly for some time, going over the conversation in her mind. She was too stimulated to sleep, but now at least she might be able to read. She picked up *Middlemarch,* turned back to where she had started skimming. Something caught her attention.

> Here Raffles rose and stalked once or twice up and down the room, swinging his leg, and assuming an air of masterly meditation. At last he stopped opposite Bulstrode and said, "I'll tell you what! Give us a couple of hundreds—come that's modest —and I'll go away—honour bright!—pick up my portmanteau and go away . . . Have you any money with you?"

She reread the passage, all thoughts of sleep forgotten.

When breakfast was brought in, she was calling New York again. Dale's voice was different, weary—of course, it was later in her working day. Beth said that she'd had a few more thoughts— "and one more thing I meant to ask."

"What's that?" Dale sounded wary.

"Where's Ollie now? I'd like to talk to him."

"I'm afraid Ollie's not available," said Dale. She didn't sound surprised at the question. She almost seemed to have been waiting for it.

"Not available?"

"He died of AIDS several years ago."

"Then can you tell me—what was the offbeat thing Ollie did?"

"Oh, the offbeat line." Again, unsurprised. "He saw *The Philadelphia Story* and went wild over Hepburn's clothes. That sent him off into a forties movies look, just for a while. Then he tossed it. . . . I know what you're thinking," said Dale. "And you're right. Her whole Silvery Screen line was from Ollie."

"Did you ever talk to Ellie about it?"

"No, I did feel uncomfortable"—Dale's voice had lost its cool— "but Ollie was dead. And Ellie was alive—and we were dear friends. So I rationalized. I told myself this was Ellie's celebration of Ollie. Maybe I should have said something, but it was just one aberration. The later stuff was all hers. So I was right—wasn't I?—not to make a thing about it. . . . But . . . with Ellie's pride in originality and her indignation about copying, it was . . . ironic."

"Yes," said Beth, "ironic."

CHAPTER
20

FRIDAY, EARLY EVENING

"There are really only two reasons for murder," said Beth. "Anger or fear."

"And the belief that you can get away with it," said Link. "Don't forget that."

"Which was the reason for Zip?" said Sig.

They were on the cocktail terrace. The staff, unusually subdued, moved unsmilingly between tables, but the guests seemed oblivious to any tensions. A group of Hawaiian dancers was the evening's entertainment, and some of the guests, among them Twinky and Doc and Burt and Suzy, had joined them in a hula.

"Fear," said Beth.

"Fear? Of what?"

"Remember our first dinner, when I mentioned I'd overheard a conversation on my lanai? It was Ellie—Eleanor—Lunette I heard." She told them about the remark that had imprinted itself on her mind. " 'I mean the chutzpah was so colossal . . . colossal!' " Beth quoted. "And that," she said, "is what got me thinking about Eleanor and Zip."

"I don't get it," said Link.

So Beth explained that she'd heard the tennis assistant repeat the *chutzpah* phrase—"and Gail said she'd picked it up from Zip. See what I mean?"

They looked baffled.

"Don't you see? Zip must have picked up the phrase from Eleanor. He must have been listening, too—outside her room."

"Isn't that stretching it?" said Link. "He could have heard it anywhere."

"Maybe, but *chutzpah* seems very atypical for a tennis pro."

"The word's all over now—even a book title."

"Not that particular combination—*chutzpah* with *colossal.*"

Link still looked doubtful.

"Anyway," said Sig, "except for Room Service, bellhops, people like that, employees aren't allowed up on the floors without authorization."

"I doubt that would apply to Zip," said Beth. "Or if it did, he could easily have invented some reason."

"Let's play along," said Link. "Say he was outside her room. What does that mean?"

"I wondered about that too." She told them about the break in Eleanor's conversation. Then she told them about her call to Dale, their agreement that Eleanor's abrupt mood change came after the interruption. "I thought it was likely that Zip was the interruption and that Eleanor's sudden dejection had something to do with him—what, I didn't know. I couldn't sleep, so I picked up *Mid-*

dlemarch, and then I got to a crucial part. It suddenly struck me—
that's the explanation."

"What part was that?" said Link.

"Bulstrode and Raffles."

"Bulstrode and Raffles! Far out—I think I know what you're
getting at."

"Well, I don't," said Sig. "Who the hell are Bulstrode and Raffles? They sound like a pair of stand-up comics."

"Bulstrode is a very religious, highly respected banker."

"A respectable banker?" said Sig. "That *is* suspicious. Who's
Raffles?"

"An old reprobate who threatens to reveal something so disgraceful from Bulstrode's past that his reputation will be destroyed—unless Bulstrode pays him off."

"I get it—a blackmailer. But what does that have to do with the
Lunette woman?"

"I think that Zip was blackmailing her—that she didn't fall—
she jumped, because she didn't see any way out."

*"If we thought a bit, of the end of it, when we started painting the
town."* The music had changed. Bruce and Carlotta were on the
floor, performing an elegant fox-trot to her favorite song.

"Zip Heinz a blackmailer!" said Sig. "That's impossible."

At dinner Link asked, "What could he have been blackmailing her
about?"

"Stealing," said Beth. Link looked up from his curry. "Yes, stealing. Some years back, Eleanor copied a line of clothes." She told
them the story. "I think that Zip found out."

"What's a little copying?" said Sig.

"Why is it," Beth said coldly, "that everyone takes copying so
lightly?"

"Hey . . . lighten up. We've all copied some way. I hear a

joke, tell it to someone else, forget to mention where I heard it. Is that so bad?"

"I'm not talking about jokes, Sig. I'm talking about original ideas, important discoveries—and the pervasive belief that it's okay to appropriate them. Look what happens. A university dean plagiarizes someone else's article into his big speech. A famous psychoanalyst wins acclaim for a book that lifts passages from a psychiatrist's scholarly study. A scientist takes credit for a virus someone else has isolated."

"I still say, what's the big deal? There are a lot worse crimes to get excited about—drugs, rape. May I have the rolls?"

"It *is* rape!" She almost threw the basket at him. "Rape of the mind! I see it, I like it—I'll take it. I'll make the millions, I'll get the honors. Forget that the glory comes from someone else's sweat, someone else's blood—"

"Someone else's wastebasket full of rewrites," said Link, "someone else's three packs of cigarettes a day. You're right, Professor," he said, giving her a look and a smile that under other circumstances might have flustered her.

She smiled back.

"Okay," said Sig. "She's right—glad you darlings are getting along so well. Still, I don't know anything about clothes—"

"But you know what you like?" Link broke in.

"But I do know"—ignoring Link—"that in the fashion industry everyone copies. They call it 'knocking off' and I've never heard of anyone going to jail for it. You're not eating."

"I'm not hungry. This was different," said Beth. "Eleanor said herself that if the designer who copied had won an award for those designs it would be . . . *murder.*" She paused, waiting for their gasps of excitement. They went on eating. "Eleanor Lunette won the FASH Award for her Silvery Screen line. It was that award that made her career take off. If her copying had become public knowledge, she would have lost everything—her future as a designer, her reputation."

"You're implying," said Link, "that she had a reason to murder Zip. This may be stating the obvious, but she could hardly have killed him, since she was dead before he was."

"True, but what if . . ." She hesitated. She had made some inroads, but they were never going to believe this.

"What if what?" said Sig, fork poised over his abalone.

"What if Eleanor wasn't the only victim? What if Zip had been blackmailing other guests? What if he had been blackmailing our little group?"

They looked over at the reunion table. Its occupants, deep in a discussion with the wine steward, had never looked happier.

"I don't believe it," said Sig. "Do they look like blackmail victims?"

"Not now. But think about the last few days. Remember Bruce—throwing the wine bottle, burning the fifty? Remember Twinky's joke on Burt? It was mean, Sig, and it's not like Twinky to be mean. And how about Burt's outburst at Suzy? Completely unlike him. He always holds in his anger even when you know he's furious. They've all been under tension."

"What could they be blackmailed about?" said Sig. "Burt, a distinguished tax lawyer. Twinky, brilliantly successful in advertising. Doc, honored in her field. Bruce and Carlotta, rolling in it. Look at them. They have everything."

"Exactly. So did Eleanor."

"What dreadful secrets could they be concealing?" said Link. "Bruce buys his clothes on sale? Twinky steals from petty cash? Carlotta shoplifts?" They looked over again, just as Carlotta put some petits fours in her bag. They started to laugh. "And Burt," said Link, carried away with his fictions. "Burt makes obscene phone calls." They roared and said what about Suzy? "Suzy? She looks up the numbers for him. First time Weather ever got an obscene phone call."

"What about Doc?" Beth asked between gales of laughter.

"Doc? She gets stock tips from her patients and gives them to Twinky. Betrayal of doctor-patient confidentiality."

"You're assuming," Beth said thoughtfully, "that they all have secrets. It could be only one for each couple. Like the Bulstrodes. He was the one with the secret. His wife didn't know. She was proud of him. If someone has been concealing a secret from a spouse, that person might have even more reason to pay off."

"It couldn't be that bad."

"It was for Mrs. Bulstrode." Beth reached into her bag.

"My God," said Sig. "She brought her book to dinner. Is that what you academics do? Read out loud to each other?"

"Ever go to an MLA convention?" Beth flipped through to the page she wanted. "Now just listen to what happens after Mrs. Bulstrode finds out about her husband."

She locked herself in her room. She needed time to get used to her maimed consciousness, her poor lopped life . . . a very searching light had fallen on her husband's character, and she could not judge him leniently: the twenty years in which she had believed in him and venerated him . . . came back with particulars that made them seem an odious deceit. He had married her with that bad past life hidden behind him and she had no faith left to protest his innocence of the worst that was imputed to him. Her honest ostentatious nature made the sharing of a merited dishonour as bitter as it could be to any mortal.

"Lots of long words," said Sig, "but gets the ideas across. Impressive. Who's the writer?" Beth told him. "I've never seen a George Eliot on the bestseller list."

"You've been looking at the wrong years," said Link. "Check out, what—the 1870s?"

"Very good—1872," said Beth.

"Oh, *literature,*" said Sig, echoing Dot, Beth thought, though he and the English department secretary could hardly have been more different. Two great people, but Dot was so much gutsier.

"By the way," Sig was saying, "whatever happened with Bulstrode and Raffles?"

"Bulstrode murdered him," said Beth.

"Murder by default, really," said Link.

"He knew," said Beth. "He helped it along. It was murder."

The adjacent bar was crowded and noisy, but on the Raffia terrace there was a heavenly quiet. A sweet, balmy breeze set the candles flickering. The scent of plumeria filled the air until Sig lit his cigar.

"The Royal," Beth was saying, "is the ideal environment for a blackmailer. People return over and over—plenty of time to get to know them, plenty of time for someone who wants to, to build up a wad of damaging information."

"Are you saying that Zip deliberately asked questions?" said Sig.

"He wouldn't have been so obvious. All he had to do was encourage them to talk. Zip was a friendly guy, wasn't he?" Sig nodded. "Can't you imagine? You take a lesson, you sit down with him afterward, schmooze awhile—a perfect time to let down, to confide. You said yourself, Sig, this is the kind of place where people open up. Zip could have helped it along, directing the conversation, probing for weaknesses. Maybe he was a good guesser—he was bound to hit it right some of the time."

"If they were blackmailed at the hotel," said Link, "why did they keep coming back?"

"*We* see the hotel as the common denominator, but they might not have had reason to. What if they weren't blackmailed here?

Zip could have been blackmailing them at home. What if this time Zip was under some kind of pressure . . . Sig, did he need money?"

"God, I don't know. He does—did—have investments. I remember in '87, when the brokers were checking out in droves, Zip said he got out just in time. . . . I don't know about recently. The market's not so good lately."

"Say he does need money—right away—so for the first time he blackmails at the hotel. It's easy to see why he picks Eleanor. She's been here many times, but she's a loner, so he thinks it's unlikely she'll confide in anyone. When Eleanor falls through"— good pun, said Link—"he thinks he'll try the others. Maybe he's desperate—or arrogant. Or both. Whatever, he decides he can get away with blackmailing them here. But he's wrong. Someone figures out the hotel connection. Someone in the group figures out it's Zip. Good-bye Zip."

Sig looked dazed. "What about the boys from the Honolulu home?"

"I never believed in that theory," said Beth.

"Why are you so sure it's someone in the group?" said Link.

"Because they're the ones with the motive."

"Then why are they so relaxed?"

"Maybe they're having a better time now—they're not being blackmailed."

"Does that mean," said Sig, "that they all know—knew—about Zip? Assuming you're right about him, which I'm not at all sure you are."

"Could be that one of them knew, could be some, could be all. That's something we have to find out."

"What do you mean, 'we'?" said Sig.

"How did he do it?" said Link. "Blackmail them at home—and here?"

"Let's not worry about methods yet," said Beth. "First we have to find out what they're concealing."

"What's this 'we' business?" Sig repeated.

"We," said Beth, "are going to team up and do some detecting."

"Detecting!" Sig took a stiff drink of his brandy. "Forget it."

"Come on, Sig," said Link. He sounded excited, eager. "It will do you good."

"Do me good! I'm too old for Hardy Boys adventures. I read the other day that after a certain age the brain starts shrinking."

"I have here," said Beth, "a clipping."

"What is it with this woman? Books, clippings—"

"Today's advice in the *Honolulu Advertiser* from the Reverend Paul Osumi—"

The best way to tell whether you are getting old is to see whether your curiosity batteries are running down. Are you curious and eager to learn about new things? Are you interested in meeting new people and making new friends? Do you keep alert to other people's ideas? Do you get enthusiastic about new happenings? After all, your real age is the state of your mind.

Sig groaned. "I think the Reverend Osumi has something else in mind—a course in computers, a date with a widow."

"Nonsense," said Link. "This is perfect. You'll learn about new things. You'll be alert to new ideas."

"Then it's decided," said Beth. "I'll take Twinky and Doc. Link" —he gave her a salute—"I'm assigning you Bruce and Carlotta."

"Why them?"

"You know all about high living. Sig, since you're a lawyer, I'm giving you Burt and Suzy."

"Fine," said Sig. "I'll start next week."

"Sig! We start tomorrow—and I'm giving you Zip too. See

what you can find out. Did he have money problems? Oh—and was he up on the floors that day?"

"Wait! I don't want to do it at all—and you're giving me three."

"It's not that rigid. We'll help each other along."

"I can feel my cholesterol going up, just thinking about it," said Sig.

"That's not your cholesterol," said Link. "That's your curiosity batteries getting a charge."

"All right. I'll do it. But the first time there's trouble—and I feel trouble coming—I'm out." He finished the brandy.

"Good," said Beth. She threw a hand in the air and slapped Link's palm.

"Come on, Sig." She threw up a hand. For a second he held back—then his chubby palm met hers.

"Isn't that lady from Chicago?" said the maître d' from the Raffia. He was looking out at the terrace, watching the exchange of high fives.

"I believe she is," said the hostess.

"She must go to a lot of Bulls games."

CHAPTER
21

SATURDAY

It had seemed like a good idea last night. Link had run into Bruce after dinner, and when Bruce asked him to play golf, he had accepted eagerly. Fits right into my assignment, he'd thought. Today Beth's plan seemed like kid stuff. He liked Beth—*admit it, you're attracted to her*—her looks, her laugh, her down-to-earth intelligence, so different from other academics he'd met. But in the light of day her theory seemed absurd. Blackmail among the palms. Crazy. And now here he was, locked into a round of golf when he'd far rather be on the beach, finishing today's stint. He had some plot problems that were giving him hell.

Thinking these gloomy thoughts, he left the hotel and made his way to the golf pro shop. On the back terrace, where people were sitting over coffee, a bearded man at a table with two women was holding forth loudly: "Intellectuals? Ha! This is the Royal, for God's sake, the kind of place where people read Judith Krantz and Lincoln Lowenstein in *hardcover*!"

"Shhh, that's him," said one of the women.

"Wow!" said the other woman. "Is he handsome or what?"

Link strode past, pretending not to hear. This, on top of the review his agent had thought fit to send him yesterday. The lines still burned in his mind—"Rags to riches plus Beauty overcomes the Beast. Anyone could follow that tired formula." His agent had scrawled a note—"What does he know?"

What, indeed, did the reviewer know, about clear, unadorned writing, about telling a story with a plot that looked outward, not inward at the writer's belly button. For that matter, what did he know about researching, working in some serious issues, even if it was pop lit. He wondered if Beth had started his book yet.

His mood worsened at the first tee. Nearby, the crowd at the practice tee gave the place a tournament atmosphere, everyone waiting, it seemed, to watch them tee off.

Bruce's ball went straight for 240 yards.

Link sliced into the rough.

After that, Link's game went downhill, steadily and dependably, consistent only in its slicing and hooking. Carlotta was no help. She couldn't sit still a minute. When they were waiting to play, she jumped out of the cart to search for lost balls. When they were playing, she drove the cart as if she owned the fairway, speeding after Bruce's ball right into Link's line of vision.

On the fifth hole, a tough par-five, he hit a mediocre drive that actually went straight. "Great shot," Bruce said patronizingly. Link fought on, hitting against the wind, and made par. "Bruce got an eagle on this one yesterday," said Carlotta.

Link took a deep breath. He looked around, at the peaceful fairways, at the glittering Pacific. Here he was, on the world's most beautiful golf course, with the world's two most annoying people. Why had he done this to himself? How, even if they were concealing something, which he fervently doubted, could he uncover it under these circumstances?

But he had to try something, Link thought, and when there was a wait at the seventh hole, he got out of his cart and went over to them. "Terrible about Zip," he said. Terrible, they agreed. "What do you think?" he asked.

There was a silence. "I heard the police are looking for some boys from a Honolulu home," Bruce said finally. "Someone off the property. What else could it have been? Terrific pro—nice guy." Said with little enthusiasm, Link thought.

"He did have a temper," said Carlotta. "Just once, Bruce gave him a stock tip that went sour. You would have thought—"

Bruce interrupted. "I think I see a ball down there, Carlotta."

"Where?" She jumped out of the cart.

To hell with curiosity batteries. I'm old, Sig thought, and that's that. Last night he had felt raring to go. This morning he had awakened early, thinking of his office, the barren desk, the phone that rang so seldom now. Too old, too old. The phrase rang through his mind. I'm not made for detecting. "To hell with curiosity batteries," he said out loud. He picked up the phone and made an appointment for a massage.

He ran into Gail in the lobby. "You sure have a lot of mail," he said, eyeing her armload of letters, magazines, newspapers from all over.

"There's still so much coming in for Zip," she said sadly.

For a moment something tugged at Sig's mind. He shrugged the thought away.

He felt more depressed than ever when he was greeted by a masseur he had never seen before. "You're new," he blurted out. "What happened to Oscar?"

"Oscar's off—he only works three days now."

Nothing ever stays the same, Sig thought, and let out a sigh.

"Feeling tired?" said the masseur. "This will pick you up."

Such solicitude—as if I've got one foot in the grave. Sig stripped and lay down on the table. "How do you like it here?" he asked indifferently.

"Oh, the Royal's great—this is pure coconut oil I'm putting on you—a high-class clientele. Not like"—he named another hotel down the coast. "All nooveeos there."

"Nooveeos?" Sig repeated. His thoughts had turned to last night's exuberant exchange of high fives.

"You know, nooveeo rich. Oh, we get a few here. You know the kind—go out of their way to let you know they have money —designer beach bags, ice-cube rocks. They're not so bad—just let your head rest in my hands—some of them give tips bigger than life. It's the repulsive ones that get to me."

"What's repulsive?" Sig asked automatically, his mind on Beth and Link. They were probably hot on the trail.

"Someone totally obese—you know, a major blubber case, comes up from the beach sweaty, greasy, without stopping to shower."

"People actually do that?" Beth probably thought he was with Suzy and Burt.

"Believe it. Just had someone come up from the fitness room, wanted me to work out a cramp. You'd think a world-class lawyer like Mr. Breneman—relax, you're tense—would know to shower first. He ran out so fast he didn't even leave a tip. Said he was in a hurry—breathe deep, visualize your muscles relaxing— had to meet his wife at the pool."

Oh well, if it just falls into my lap I suppose I'm obligated. Sig sat up.

"You have more time coming, Mr. Winterfield. I'm not finished."

"That's all right—just thought of something I forgot to do." Sig stumbled into his shorts.

"Thank *you*, Mr. Winterfield." The bill disappeared like a sleight of hand trick. "Wait—you forgot your watch."

The masseur watched Sig scuttle out. Strange old guy. That watch must have cost a bundle. That's where all the money is—senior citizens, filthy rich, but they don't mind collecting social security. When it's my turn, there won't be anything left.

"What floor?" said Sig as an attractive young woman stepped into the elevator with him.

"You're the new operator?" she joked.

"I'm accepting tips," he said, surprised at how cheerful he felt. He couldn't wait to change and get down to the pool.

"You were awesome," said Beth's new partner, shaking hands energetically. Lanky legs easily clearing the net, he reached out to Twinky and Doc.

"I don't mind being slaughtered when my opponent is the former captain of the Yale tennis team," said Twinky, and went to get drinks. "Jon, you stay and charm the ladies."

Beth left it to Doc to keep the conversation going, while she sat watching the players on the adjacent court. How unreal everything was. Just a few days ago their group had gathered around this table, talking to Zip. Now Zip was gone, but the tennis went on. She wondered what Sig and Link were doing and hoped they were making more progress than she was.

"Beth teaches at Midwestern," Doc was saying.

"Their J-school is awesome," said Jon, and started asking Beth about Midwestern.

A nice kid, she thought, but I wish he'd leave. If she were alone with Twinky and Doc, she could direct the conversation to Zip. She answered Jon's questions automatically, all the while watching Twinky out of the corner of her eye. He had passed the drinks machine and was standing outside Zip's office. He tried the door, then moved to the window, and stood for some time looking inside.

When Twinky returned, Doc was asking Jon his plans after his year off. "Grad school, probably," he said, "but it's incredibly up for grabs. Maybe journalism, maybe business—I'm thinking about advertising. That's your field, Mr. Delorio."

"Hey—call me Twinky. We don't go formal here."

"Okay, Twinky. Say, I heard you won the Claudia for my favorite commercial. I was taking a twentieth-century U.S. history course at the time, and the prof even mentioned the way you really caught the spirit of the Rough Riders following T.R. into the charge. How do you get your ideas?"

"Lots of ways. Sometimes they come when a bunch of us are sitting around talking. Sometimes we bring newspapers and try to take advantage of what's going on in the world. During an election year we might use a takeoff on the candidates."

"I see," said Jon. "Like right now you might do something with the Supreme Court, maybe all the justices in their robes—they could be concurring on a decision."

"Great idea," said Twinky. "Hang on a sec." He borrowed scratch paper from the tennis desk and made some notes.

"Do you really think you might do something with my idea?"

"Probably not." Jon looked disappointed. "Hey," said Twinky, "before a campaign we might develop ten or fifteen ideas—most of them get tossed. I'll let you know if anything comes of it."

Doc moved suddenly and knocked her drink off the table. Jon brought towels, and after the mopping up was complete, he said to Twinky, "Is that how you came up with the T.R. commercial? A whole group throwing ideas around?"

"Not that one," Twinky said firmly. "I was working through some stuff at home and the idea just popped into my head. Then I researched it—I must have hit every book on T.R.—and the rest, as they say, is history. Never dreamed it would click so well. Especially since it took some doing to convince the client. I made the presentation at a lunch meeting—I wrote all over the table-cloth showing him how it could work."

"Awesome. What's it like at a top agency?"

"Well, Jon, there are the generals and there are the foot soldiers. The generals are the creative directors—the top strategists. The foot soldiers—copywriters and art directors—report to the creative director. . . ." Twinky went on and on interminably. Doc fidgeted in her chair, playing with the zipper on her racket cover.

"Well," Jon said finally, "great talking to you."

"Come and see me when you finish grad school," said Twinky. "We're always looking for new talent."

"Do you mean it? Awesome. Congrats again on your Claudia. Good thing McKinley was shot, huh?"

Twinky looked perplexed. "McKinley? . . . Oh, yeah, good thing."

"I'm going too," said Doc. She sounded low. "I'm due at the beauty shop in fifteen minutes."

"Me too," Beth said instantly. "See you there."

Beth went to the tennis desk, waited until Doc was out of ear-shot, then called for an appointment, saying she had to get in right away. Before she left she took a quick look through the window of Zip's office—packed walls, overflowing shelves, filled with trophies and a motley collection of souvenirs, even a stuffed bear in a tennis outfit, its furry arms holding—she peered—it looked like a restaurant menu.

They had reached the famous ninth hole. On a promontory, the elevated tee overlooked a deep inlet where water rushed in. The ball had to be driven over the inlet and onto a very fast green.

"I'm not ready yet," said Bruce, fumbling for something in his bag. "Why don't you hit first."

Link looked down at the water and across to the slope where vicious rocks barred the way to the green. Only a psychological handicap, he told himself. He eyed the flag, took a few practice swings. "Good luck, Link," said Carlotta. He wanted to throw his club at her.

He swung. The ball moved up, up—hit the rocks and careened into the water. "Almost," Carlotta said cheerfully. Link wondered if he could hire the murderer to get rid of her.

"Got it over three out of the last three times," said Bruce. He teed up, swung—they watched his ball soar over the water and touch down on the green. Bruce grinned at Link. "Guess my luck is holding."

"Or else," said Link, "nine is a hot number for you."

"Nine?" said Bruce.

"You know, the ninth hole. For me it's still a due number—like all the other holes."

"What's this 'hot number, due number' business?" said Bruce.

"Oh, nothing," Link said with inward triumph. "I'm really just saying that you understand the mechanical bias of this hole."

"Mechanical bias?" Bruce looked thoroughly confused.

"Come on," said Carlotta. "Let's stop for a snack."

"Terrific idea," said Link. For the first time, he was really enjoying himself.

"*Up,* back, around and down. *Up,* back, around and down." The women clung to the side of the pool and bobbed obediently.

Sig threw his robe on a lounge and looked around. Where the devil were Suzy and Burt? Except for the exercise class, the pool was devoid of swimmers.

"Want me to put the umbrella up for you, Mr. W.?"

"That's okay." He'd spotted them. Walking at a desperate pace,

Sig cursed himself for not wearing sandals and winced each time bare foot hit hot stone. At last he gained the top step of the Jacuzzi, where Suzy, eyes closed, leaned back languidly, while Burt expounded to a young woman. "If Anita Hill had a real case," he was saying, "why did she wait so long to make her accusations?"

"Who would have believed her? He was the senior person. He was the one with the power."

"Come on in, Sig," said Burt. "The water's fine." Gingerly, Sig went down the steps, moved through the bubbles, and took the spot next to Suzy. "Let me introduce Jojo," said Burt. "She's first year law at Stanford. We're talking about the Thomas hearings. And why"—turning back to Jojo—"if she was so harassed, did she follow him from place to place?"

"It was the logical thing to do. She was ambitious—and like I said, he was the one with the power."

It was a discussion Sig had heard many times, and he wished they'd get off it. Water bubbled around his legs, as he thought about how he would frame his talk with Burt. He could begin by working Zip into the conversation.

"Men still have all the power," said Jojo, kicking out into the bubbles. "How many women in your firm are senior partners?"

"I'll be honest with you," said Burt. "Not that many. But you women have got to pay your dues like everyone else. You'd see more women senior partners if more women were full-time. I don't believe in this Mommy Track, half-time business. You can't be a lawyer unless you're available whenever your clients need you."

"Yeah, but isn't it great"—the voice was Twinky's—"to be able to say to some well-educated young woman"—he jumped in, creating a minor tidal wave, and came up with water streaming over his face—"go research this for me . . . ? Well, isn't it, Burt?"

Suzy, who had looked up at Twinky's arrival, closed her eyes again.

"Isn't what?" said Burt.

"Great to have some bright young woman do your research?"

"*Up,* down, twirl. *Up,* down, twirl." In the pool, the women bobbed and turned.

"You should get into that class, Suzy. You need the workout."

"Oh, Burt, it starts so early."

"I bet *you* do great research, Jojo." Twinky kicked out at her playfully.

"How many cases," said Jojo, ignoring Twinky, "really require full-time availability to the client?"

Let's see, Sig thought, I could ask if he had taken lessons from Zip this time.

"Another thing," said Burt. "What about women who go on maternity leave and never come back? Most women are not really dedicated. But that doesn't stop them from taking a job from a man with a family to support."

Or, Sig thought, I could ask if he kept in touch with Zip during the year. But is that too direct?

"Did you ever think, Jojo"—Twinky made another effort to get her attention—"a Jacuzzi is really a modern version of the Old West. A little group in a circle, talking—the way people used to gather around the campfire, swapping stories."

"What cases exactly require full-time work?" Jojo snapped at Burt.

"Show some respect," said Twinky. "Do you know who you're talking to?" Jojo shook her head. "Burton Breneman of the Breneman loophole—saved me a bundle on taxes. Burt, what did you publish in? I know it was one of those big-time law journals."

"Getting too hot," Suzy said suddenly. "I'm going in the pool. Then let's have some lunch, Burt. I'm starving."

"After that breakfast you put away?"

Jojo looked from Burt to Suzy. "I'll join you, Suzy," she said. "I'm getting hot, too, and it's not the water."

"No offense, I hope," said Burt. "I'm just saying that women have got to get their tickets punched too. You know it's like. . . ."

"And I'm saying," Jojo threw back, "that they can get their tickets punched forever, but men will never give up their power."

Twinky, who had been eyeing Jojo's bikinied figure ever since she had emerged, went up the steps. At last Sig had his chance. He looked ahead, absently watching Suzy do laps, and said, "I've been meaning to ask you, Burt—"

"Sig Winterfield! Just the man I want!" Standing above them, Sig saw with horror, was a woman from the exercise class. God, he couldn't remember her name, but he remembered her all too well. "Sig, I want to introduce you"—he listened, panic rising—"to someone"—her voice had a hustler's zeal—"very, very special."

Damn. Behind her stood another woman of ample bosom and years. She was smiling—humorously? angrily? Whatever, she looked as reluctant as he felt. Still, long experience had taught Sig that it would take all his wits to overcome the iron matchmaking instincts of what's-her-face. Courtesy required he get out of the Jacuzzi. He stood talking with them, switching from hotfoot to hotfoot, willing Burt to stay put.

But the evasive action took longer than he had hoped, and by the time he had extricated himself Burt was out of the Jacuzzi and he and Suzy had departed.

"Kick, kick, kick! That's just great!" The instructor's voice had taken on the high, saccharine tone she used for teaching children. "Kick, kick, kick! Great! You closed your mouth! Tah-ri-fic!"

Yeah, terrific. And what would he have to report at dinner tonight?

*　*　*

The hairdresser looked over Doc's shoulder. "You're reading the personals!"

"Silly things," Doc said, and put the magazine down, almost guiltily.

"Oh, I love them," said the hairdresser. "Especially the match-making ones in *Gotham*. Listen to this: 'Interesting, single white male. Tall, six feet four inches, enjoys travel—"

"Ouch," said Suzy.

"You moved your foot, Mrs. Breneman," the pedicurist said re-proachfully.

" 'And vigorous outdoor activity. Seeking intelligent, successful young woman, 42-24-35 . . .' How about those measurements? What does he want?" the hairdresser asked the salon. "Dolly Parton?" She looked around for a response.

The only comment came from Carlotta. "Oh, my God," she said, peering into the mirror. "I think I'm breaking out."

Disappointed, the hairdresser handed the magazine to Doc, who refused it.

Beth was shampooed and ushered to the booth between Doc and Carlotta. To her left, Carlotta was giving instructions—"fuller on the sides, higher on top"—and talking about golf. She had left Bruce in the middle of a fantastic round. To her right, the hair-dresser was telling Doc about her back problem. "I wish I had a woman doctor," she said, "someone I could really talk to. Like you."

"She's wonderful," Suzy announced to the salon. "Last year Burt thought he was having a heart attack, and Doc examined him. They were in the nurse's office—Burt made me leave—and they were there so long I was terrified. Thank God, it wasn't his heart. It was—what was it, Doc?"

"Chest wall pain," Doc said in a low, clipped voice.

"That's it. Burt," she informed the salon, "used to say it was a waste of time to send women to medical school, but when he came out of that room—well, he couldn't say enough about Doc. 'Knows what she's doing, really listens,' " Suzy said, as if a compliment from Burt was the greatest accolade a woman could receive.

"Twinky thinks I spend too much time with patients."

"Well, Burt doesn't." Suzy paused to confer about polish color. Then she said, "Where *is* Twinky?"

"Holed up in the room—working on a new campaign."

If he was working on a new campaign, Beth thought, it was not advertising. On the way over, as she passed the pool, she had seen Twinky talking to a superb-looking young woman in a bikini.

"Burt's in the room, too, working up a talk. I had to leave because I was interfering with his concentration. He's made me do so much walking, my feet are ruined—so I thought, why not another pedicure." There was pride in Suzy's voice as she made these comments, not even a tinge of resentment, thought Beth, at Burt's jurisdiction over her every action.

The hairdresser turned the dryer on Beth's hair, and the voices —and any relevant information—were smothered. Oh, well. She picked up *Middlemarch*. The book fell open to an early section, and my God, here was Doc: "Adoring her husband's virtues, she had very early made up her mind to his incapacity of minding his own interests and had met the consequences cheerfully." And a few pages on: "A woman, let her be as good as she may, has got to put up with the life her husband makes for her." The very picture of Suzy.

Then Beth laughed at herself for this constant transposing of nineteenth-century England to Hawaii. She was getting like that character in *The Moonstone* who opened *Robinson Crusoe* at random, whenever he wanted insight or advice. But it *was* uncanny, she thought, as the girl swiveled the chair around and held up a hand mirror. All that was lacking was a description of Carlotta's relationship with Bruce.

After the great good luck of finding all three women together, Beth thought as she left the salon, she had learned nothing. Still thinking about how little progress she had made, she took a different turn and realized she was in a part of the hotel she had never seen. Ahead, double doors were open to what resembled an enormous family room. A television was on. Children sprawled over huge sofas, watching cartoons. Some bookshelves on the far wall caught her eye, and she went over to look. Among ancient bestsellers and tattered *Reader's Digest* condensed books was a children's encyclopedia from a publisher now defunct. She chose a volume and began to read. When someone came to shoo the children outside, she hardly noticed. For the first time, she felt a surge of excitement. She might not be any closer to the murderer, but now at least she had proof that the motive she had guessed at existed.

As she returned the volume to the shelf, another thought struck her. She looked at her watch—just enough time before dinner.

They were closing the pro shop when Beth rushed through to the courts. She went directly to Zip's office and looked through the window. She stood motionless, fascinated with the objects on the desk and the shelves. Once, she had a vague sense she was being watched, and she turned to look. The shop was closed. The courts were empty. She was certain she was alone.

CHAPTER
22

The Buddha looked especially beautiful tonight, gazing down serenely at the people strolling into the Islands Room. A lovely room, double-leveled, ringed with windows, it was less formal than the other dining rooms, but with the same shipboard feeling. More important, the Islands Room specialized in regional Hawaiian cuisine. They had decided to meet here because they were sure the others would choose the more glamorous Raffia, especially since Twinky and Burt were steak and rack-of-lamb types.

Beth, looking forward to comparing notes, walked in eagerly. Sig and Link were already there. Unfortunately, so was the reunion group. Bad luck. Still, the tables were far enough apart so they could talk without being overheard.

"Who's going to start?" said Beth, after drink orders were taken.

"How about you?" Link suggested, "since you look so lovely tonight."

She smiled and said she would rather wait.

"I'll start then," said Link, "but I don't have that much. I was up bright and early to play golf." He paused, remembering the galling remark he had overheard. "I had a rotten round."

"Of course you did," said Beth. "You were detecting."

"Sherlock Holmes would have detected *and* made a hole in one."

"He had Watson to caddy for him . . . never mind. What did you find out?"

"That Bruce is a great golfer. . . . Okay, okay. I found out that Zip may have needed money if he was still playing the market." He told them what Carlotta had said about the stock tip that went sour.

"Is that it?" said Beth.

"No," he said with more enthusiasm, "it is not. Sig, didn't you say Bruce had a system for winning the lottery?"

"That's the story he gave out."

"Well, the systems man knows zip—forgive the pun—about systems. I happen to have done some research—I'm thinking of using lottery winners in a novel—and you can take it from me, there is no such thing as a winning system. But that's not what matters. What matters . . ." He waved as Carlotta and Bruce went to the dance floor. "What matters," he said in a lower voice, "is that Bruce doesn't even know the vocabulary. He's never heard of due numbers. He's never heard of hot numbers. And he doesn't have a clue about mechanical bias."

"Wait!" Sig and Beth said together.

"All right, all right . . . Due numbers are numbers that haven't come up for a long time and are therefore supposedly due. Hot numbers are numbers that have been coming up frequently."

"And mechanical bias?" said Beth.

"Oh that. A machine could have some minor peculiarity that makes some numbers come up more often than others. And some balls, depending on how old they are, could roll faster and make certain numbers come up more often."

"So if you knew," said Beth, "which machine or which balls would be used, you could predict some numbers and—"

"Forget it. Illinois goes through a whole rigamarole to prevent exactly that. Before the real lottery, they have a prelottery that picks at random which machines and balls will be used. There's no way anyone could use bias to form a system. Still, if Bruce thought he had a system, he should have known those terms. Something's wrong for sure," said Link. "But I don't see that it has anything to do with what we're after."

"It has plenty to do with what we're after," said Beth, but refused to tell them just yet. "Fabulous, Link." She gave him a smile, and wondered why he had looked so unhappy earlier. "Now, Sig, what about you?"

"You go ahead."

"No, you—please. I want to be last."

Sig took several spoons of his egg flower consommé. Then he said, "Okay, nothing."

"Nothing? What did you do?"

"I got a massage."

"That has possibilities," she said doubtfully. "What did you learn?"

"Nothing—except that I don't like the new masseur. Too gossipy."

"But a gossip is exactly what we want! What a great opportunity!"

"A great opportunity to get a lousy massage. And there's something sleazy about the new masseur. You can ask Burt. The masseur told me Burt left just before I got there. He also broke the news that Burt didn't leave a tip."

"He's sleazy. He's a blabber. Perfect!" said Beth. "Sig, you've got to go back."

"I don't want to go back. Why should I?"

"So you can encourage him to dish some more dirt."

"About who?"

"All of them, any of them—didn't he tell you anything else about Burt?"

"Yeah—that he needed a shower." Beth nodded happily. "Oh, and he told me Suzy and Burt were at the pool, so I went down there."

"I knew you learned something!"

"But I didn't. The whole time we were in the Jacuzzi, Burt was talking to a knockout girl—a law student. That's it."

"That can't be all. What did they talk about?"

"The Thomas hearings. Nothing that matters. I did learn that Burt can't be winning any popularity contests with the women in his firm. He thinks women, especially married women with children, have no place in a law firm."

"You didn't ask him about Zip?"

"I intended to ask both of them, but they left before I had a chance," Sig said grumpily, thinking about his tremendous battle to avoid being fixed up. "Okay, Beth, no more stalling."

The waiter arrived with sesame shrimp with lilikoi glaze (Beth), duck curry with pineapple (Sig), linguini with macadamia pesto (Link). He passed the rolls. Then the busboy made sure their glasses were refilled. Then the waiter asked if they had everything they wanted.

"Everything!" said Sig, and looked at Beth expectantly.

"To begin with, if Bruce knows zip about systems"—she couldn't keep a note of exultation out of her voice—"Twinky, who produced a prize-winning commercial about Teddy Roosevelt, knows zip about Teddy Roosevelt." She told them about Jon's remark about McKinley, and Twinky's bewilderment, and waited for them to comment—and waited. "Okay," she said finally. "Roosevelt got into office because McKinley was assassinated. I admit I didn't get the McKinley remark either until I looked it up."

"Looked it up where?" said Sig. "Did you pack a history text too?"

"I found a children's encyclopedia—stop laughing, it gave me what I needed. And the point is, Twinky should have known about McKinley. He said he'd read everything about Roosevelt." Then she told them about Twinky's long look into Zip's office and her return visit. "On one of the shelves there was a teddy bear, holding a menu!"

"So what does that prove?" Sig said. She could tell he was feeling bad because he thought he should have come up with more.

"Teddy bears—as I learned from my reading—were named after Teddy Roosevelt. I'm sure Zip put it there to goad Twinky."

"Goad him about what?"

"Obviously something to do with the commercial."

"And the menu?"

"Probably stands for O'Connor's. And there were other things on the shelves. Significant things. A bowl of Ping-Pong balls sprinkled with glitter. A miniature oil rig. A toy cow."

"The Ping-Pong balls," said Link. "They have to symbolize the lottery. And the glitter—big winnings."

"Right. That sends a message to Bruce and Carlotta."

"What about the oil rig?" said Link. "And the cow?"

"Oil and cattle," said Sig. "Typical tax expenditures—better known as loopholes."

"Exactly—a message to Burt. I knew you'd get it, Sig."

"You're implying these were threatening messages," he said. "Maybe it was Zip's way of congratulating his friends on their success."

"Or maybe he was being sadistic," said Beth.

"Sadistic?"

"Remember those few days when they were all so on edge? I'm sure that's when Zip was blackmailing them. Remember the tennis game? No, I forgot, you two didn't get there until Twinky and Bruce had the fight. But long before that, Zip was making jibes that connect with those symbols on his shelves. When Burt hit a good shot, Zip said things like 'Well done, tax expert,' or 'Real tiger, tax expert,' and then Burt's game disintegrated. He even yelled at Suzy, and he never does that—he orders her around, but he never yells. Same thing with Twinky. He put one away and Zip called out, 'Charge, men! Just like T.R.,' and Twinky's game fell apart. Later on Carlotta told Bruce to stop poaching, and Zip said something to Bruce about sharing the glory—and then Bruce completely lost it. They all lost it. It was right after that that Twinky and Bruce started punching each other out."

"What was 'share the glory' supposed to mean?" said Link.

"I don't know, but I'd bet my—"

"Your *Middlemarch*?" Link suggested. "You'll never find another copy in the gift shop."

"Right. I'd bet my *Middlemarch* it had something to do with the lottery."

"So you think those things in his office," said Sig, "connect with the secrets he was blackmailing them about. And then in the tennis game—"

"He was deliberately torturing them."

On the dance floor, Twinky and Doc were doing a wild jitterbug, drawing as much attention as Bruce and Carlotta. At the table, Burt was putting a sweater around Suzy's bare shoulders.

"Do you think they knew it was deliberate," said Link, "that they knew he was the blackmailer?"

"Someone did," said Beth, noting with satisfaction that they no longer doubted that Zip was a blackmailer. "It was the next day that Zip was murdered."

"Which," said Sig, "brings us to the real question."

"And what is that?" said Beth.

"Who knew what and when did they know it?"

"Alohagate!" said Link.

CHAPTER
23

"Let's get back to the secrets," said Link. They had finished dinner and were sitting in the softly lit lobby, having taken possession of one of the groups of soft armchairs that surrounded the atrium. "What exactly was Zip torturing them about? What is it about the loophole and the commercial and the lottery that's so disgraceful?"

"There has to be a common denominator," said Beth.

They looked up as a group of late arrivals straggled in. Dazed with jet lag, they bent to receive leis, then staggered to the front desk, forming a line. Some carried their logo-decorated hand luggage. Others left their bags on the floor and kicked them along indifferently.

"They're all winners!" Link said loudly, making Beth jump. "Twinky won the Claudia. Eleanor won . . . What was it?"

"The FASH Award," said Beth. "And Bruce won the lottery!"—falling in with his excitement.

"Burt didn't win anything," Sig said flatly—and their exuberance was punctured. Like Bulstrode in *Middlemarch,* Beth thought, when his guilty past is discovered and his puffed-up pomposity is suddenly deflated. Of course, she and Sig and Link were guilty of nothing except trying to get at the truth.

They sat watching guests walk back and forth, some to the elevators, some down the stairs to watch the movie. The smell of popcorn wafted up, mingling agreeably with the scent of jasmine —until Sig lit a cigar, protesting that it helped him think.

"They're all originators," he said suddenly. "Eleanor created fashion designs. Twinky created a commercial. Even Burt—it takes creativity, believe me, to discover a new loophole. And Bruce—he invented a system."

"Or thought he did," said Link, stretching out his long legs on a bronze drum table.

"He did create something," said Beth, "a nonworking something, but he created it. So he's an originator. . . . too. Good for you, Sig. Great insight."

"We're agreed then," said Link. "They all created something new. But where does it get us? More important, where did it get Zip?"

"What if the ideas weren't their own?" said Sig. "What if they copied—"

"Stole," said Beth.

"From someone else—the way Eleanor copied her idea. I don't know, maybe I'm getting like you, Beth, making too much of originality."

"You can't make too much of it. It's despicable to steal someone else's ideas. More than that, if it's found out, the person who stole could be destroyed." She thought of a former friend whose life had been destroyed for that very reason, who before being found out had terrorized the Midwestern campus. "If Twinky stole and his theft was discovered, that would mean a tremendous loss of prestige. He'd have to relinquish the prize. He could lose his job."

"Burt gave talks all over the place about his loophole," said Sig, "and he published in the *National Law Journal.* All the lawyers read it. If it was found out that he stole, he'd be drummed out of his firm. And if Bruce stole . . ." Sig stopped, looking bewildered. "But what did he steal?"

They sat, thinking. An expensively dressed couple got off the elevator and went to the reception desk. They could hear the woman asking the clerk to let them into the safe-deposit room so she could put her jewels to bed.

Too bad you can't lock up an idea to keep it safe, Beth thought. But ideas have to be brought to light, tested in public. Otherwise, how to know if . . . "Bruce could have stolen an idea too," she said. "Someone else's system—someone's nonworking system. It's still an idea."

"We're doing an awful lot of conjecturing," Sig said gloomily. "Even if we're right, and they all stole, it would be impossible to find out who they stole from."

"This morning," said Beth, "Twinky was talking about foot soldiers—underlings in his agency. I know of a case where someone stole from an underling."

"Twinky certainly believes in getting other people to do the work," said Sig.

Beth asked how he knew that.

"He joined us in the Jacuzzi."

"You never mentioned it."

"I didn't think it was important. He was asking Burt, wouldn't it be great to have some bright young woman do the research for you. Of course, that's nothing new at a law firm. Seniors are always telling a younger person to go research something for them." Sig's face lit up. "Burt could have stolen from some junior person who did his research!"

"You're talking about a bunch of weaklings," said Link. "If all these people had their ideas stolen, why didn't they speak up? We know why in Eleanor's case—the guy she lifted from was dead. But they can't all be dead. Why were they so spineless?"

"Jojo!" said Sig.

"Who's Jojo?" said Link.

"You know—the law student. Burt kept riding her about why, if Clarence Thomas harassed her, Anita Hill waited years to blow the whistle on him. Jojo told him straight out. She waited because no one would have believed her—he was the senior person. That could explain what happened with Burt. If he stole from a junior person, the junior would be afraid to come forward. A junior would think, it's my word against a senior partner's—who would believe me? He could blackball me."

"Look what happened to Anita Hill when she did speak out," said Beth. "You know," she said thoughtfully, "the same could hold true for an ad agency. A younger person could feel too powerless to come forward, afraid it would backfire on her—or him."

"At an ad agency," Link said with authority, "it would be double-barreled backfire."

"You're going to use an ad agency in a novel?" said Beth.

He laughed. "I see you still haven't read my book."

"Oh, but I will! Just as soon as—"

"No rush," said Link, giving her a look so admiring, so amatory that—never mind how it made her feel, she thought, not now. . . . "If a client found out Twinky's commercial was stolen," Link was saying, "that could be good-bye O'Connor's account. Clients cancel accounts for far less important reasons. And where would that leave the person who complained that Twinky had copied his idea?"

Sig sighed. "How to prove it? How to find these people? If they exist."

"I wish I'd known all this when I followed Doc to the beauty shop," said Beth.

"You were at the beauty shop with Doc?" said Link.

"And Suzy. And Carlotta."

"What a great opportunity," said Sig, turning the tables on Beth. "What did you learn?"

"Nothing."

"But everyone gossips in a beauty shop."

"They talked, of course. But nothing came out—nothing that matters. Oh there was some discussion about personal ads. Doc said they were silly—she was reading the matchmaking ads in *Gotham*. The hairdresser started reading one out loud. It was so funny. . . ." She trailed off. No one seemed interested.

"Think I'll go up," said Sig. "I can't take these late hours."

"I'll never get to sleep," said Beth.

"Let's go for a walk," said Link. "The moon is . . . well, wait till you see it."

"Have fun, children." Sig made for the elevator.

They left their shoes on the terrace. Holding hands, they went down the stairs to the beach. Coming their way were Twinky and Doc, Doc almost dragging herself along.

"Going for a walk?" said Twinky. "Watch out for the lady in white. She's been sighted dancing on the stairway, spinning around the front circle. The fishermen on the beach have seen her walking along the trail."

"Who is she?" said Link.

"A restless spirit," Twinky said in preternatural tones. "She appears in a circle of light."

"Well, you're safe tonight," Doc said dryly. "The lady only comes out on the darkest night of the week." She sounded exhausted.

"What's the matter, Doc?" Beth asked her. "Are you sick?"

"Nothing serious," she said with professional calm. "Just a touch of nausea."

"I told you we should have gone to the Raffia," said Twinky.

"I thought some air would help," said Doc, "but I'm still feeling queasy. Think I'll have a lazy day tomorrow."

"Guess I'll be running alone," said Twinky. "Hawking dead bodies."

"That," Doc snapped, "is a disgusting joke. Grisly. Unnecessary."

But she didn't say *cruel,* Beth thought. And Zip had been their friend.

"Darling," said Twinky, unperturbed. "You know I meant golf balls." Then, telling Doc he'd meet her in the room, that he'd forgotten today's dose of good luck, he ran to rub the Buddha's belly.

CHAPTER
24

Sounds of heavy metal music roared through the open lanai. Angrily, Carlotta ripped the price tag off her nightgown, slipped it on, and strode to the phone. "I don't care—get them to stop. *Now!*"

"Speaking of complaints," Bruce called from the bathroom, "whose idea was it to eat in the Islands?"

"Mine," Carlotta admitted. "Anyway, I liked the food."

"Look what happened to Doc."

"It doesn't have to be something she ate," said Carlotta. She was at the closet, contemplating her clothes for the next day.

Bruce emerged, wrapped in a towel. "You don't sound very sympathetic, darling." He dried himself vigorously and threw the towel in the direction of the bathroom.

"Oh, sometimes Doc is just . . . too much. She exercises. She keeps up her looks. She has a career. And she's so bloody *decent,*" said Carlotta. "Never gives advice unless she's asked, always listens sympathetically—Miss Goody-goody! There are times . . . I'd like to . . . shake her." Another metallic blast. "Damn it!" Carlotta started for the phone. "My God! What's that?" She pointed to an envelope on the table.

"Jesus you're jumpy. It's the advance bill." Bruce—nude—sat down and put his feet on the table. "I see they raised the golf fees. Wow! Have I played that many rounds?"

"So what?" said Carlotta. "Why shouldn't you play as much golf as you want? Why shouldn't we do what we want? There's so much I want to do, Bruce. I want to travel more. I want to take the Orient Express to—where does it go?"

"Venice."

"Venice. I want to cruise the Greek islands. I want to take a villa in Italy."

"We will, darling, we will."

"I want to go to Paris for the collections. I want to have dinner at Tour d'Argent. I want to . . ." An ear-splitting blast. "That does it! I'm calling Bucky!"

But Bruce was at the phone ahead of her.

"Who are you calling?"

"Home—see if we have any messages."

"Why bother?"

He pushed some buttons, listened for a minute. For a split second, a troubled expression crossed his face.

"Well?"

"The Lyric. Calling for a contribution. The Symphony. Calling for a contribution. The cleaners. Offering a bargain on draperies."

"Any people calls?"

"Just Esperanza."

Carlotta made a face. "What's her problem?"

"The usual."

"Don't give her another cent!" Carlotta shouted over the music.

"And don't give me advice. I'll handle Esperanza."

"You always do, don't you?"

"What?"

"Handle things. Sometimes I can handle—" The music stopped abruptly. "Thank God," said Carlotta. "The Front Desk finally did something."

"Think of the new friends you just made," said Bruce.

"Who?"

"All the teenagers who just checked in with their families."

She shrugged.

"New nightgown?" said Bruce. "I like it."

"Do you really?"

"Maybe we should crack the champagne tonight."

"Oh . . . the champagne," she said, without enthusiasm. "Let's wait." She removed the flowers from the pillow, threw them on the floor, and stretched out next to Bruce.

"So," he said, "who do you think did it?"

"Did what?"

"You know—Zip."

"I don't know—had to be someone powerful. It must have been a man."

"Not necessarily, darling. Look at you. Quite a build"—admiring the well-toned body under the sheer nightgown.

"Oh, Bru"—she dived toward him—"you're pretty powerful yourself."

Suzy chattered on, asking the maid about her family, while the maid removed the bright spreads and swiftly made up the bed. She turned back the sheets, and placed blossoms on the pillows. Then she looked meaningfully toward the bathroom.

"Burt," Suzy called. "She needs to get in there now."

Out came Burt, wearing a short, bamboo-print *yukata* that made him look like a tree—a walking, stalking tree. He tramped around the room. "Thought I was going to be trapped in there all night! You were talking to her! Makes her take twice as long."

"Shhh, she'll hear you," as the maid carried out the used towels.

"I don't care if she does," said Burt. "You shouldn't get so friendly with the help. Before you know it, they're taking advantage of you, expecting big—" His eyes lit on the dresser. "What happened to the champagne?"

"I gave it to Keke."

"You gave it to the day maid!"

"Shhh"—as the maid reentered with fresh towels. Sounds of running water came from the bathroom.

"That was our champagne from the hotel. For what we spend, they should spend, a whole case."

"It was a celebration gift."

"Celebration! Of what?"

"She has a new baby."

"Then she should be home taking care of it."

"Sit down, Burt," Suzy said with sudden bravado.

Surprised, he did as he was told.

"Now I want you to listen to me! Not all women are as lucky as I am. I'm married to a—a celebrated lawyer."

"Now, Suzy"—looking prim—"that's overdoing it. You could say I'm respected, but not—"

"No! Celebrated! You're invited to lecture. You're given a distinguished-alumni award. You're on important boards. Your clients invite us everywhere—to their clubs, their summer homes, their yachts, box seats at the races." She giggled. "Remember when I won the daily double? But Keke. Her life—"

"Oh Keke," said Burt, losing interest. "Let her enjoy the champagne."

"Half the time her husband isn't working."

But Burt had stopped listening. He put on his glasses and picked up the hotel bill, checking each entry against his diary.

Shortly afterward the maid called good night. Suzy undressed, threw her clothes on the chair, and went into the bathroom, appearing a few minutes later in a ruffled gown, face shiny, hair in a ponytail. She sniffed the flowers on the pillow, placed them lovingly on the bedside table. Then she dropped into bed, gave a blissful sigh, and opened Link's latest book.

"I won't pay it!" said Burt. "We didn't buy anything in the clothes shop."

"Yes we did," Suzy said calmly.

"For God's sake, Suzy. What now?"

"That red outfit—I just had to have it. It's perfect for here—and for summer at home."

"You have a whole closet full of summer outfits."

"Well, why shouldn't I? The wife of a celebrated lawyer." She started to cry.

"Oh, Suzy—it's all right." He got up, went over to the bed and kissed her. "You look cute in your ponytail."

Suzy read her book. Burt finished going over the bill, folded it into the envelope, and started to get into bed. He frowned. "You're just going to leave your things there?"

Suzy yawned. "In the morning."

Burt got out of bed. He picked up Suzy's shoes and dress.

"Oh Burt, don't bother."

"You know I like the room to be shipshape." He put the shoes in the closet and hung up the dress. Seeing a package of laundry, he opened it and started putting things away.

Suzy looked up from her book. "Dear," she said, "do you have any idea . . ."

"Any idea about what?"—opening a drawer. "They ruined my best shirt!"

"You know . . . Do you have any idea who—did that—to Zip?"

"How should I know?" He slammed the drawer shut, tossed the laundry wrapper, and saw a paper pinned to it. "Suzy! Do you know how much they charged for my underwear?"

"Aloha. Housekeeping."

Twinky opened the door. "Never mind making up the room tonight," he told the maid. They both looked at the bathroom, listening to the unmistakable noises of someone retching. "I'll just take the towels," said Twinky.

A few minutes later Doc staggered out. Dizzily, she looked around the littered room, made a move as if to put things away, changed her mind and crawled into bed.

"Well!" Twinky came in from the lanai. "You've rejoined the living." He looked at her ashen face. "Guess this isn't the right night for the champagne?"

Doc torpedoed his cheerful smile with a scowl. "There will never," she said angrily, "be a right night for the champagne." Suddenly she flung out of bed.

When she came out of the bathroom again, she opened her medicine case and took out a small bottle. "What's that?" said Twinky, watching her swallow a small green pill.

"Something to relieve the nausea," she replied from the bed, her voice like a winter freeze.

"Did it help?" said Twinky.

"It will be at least fifteen minutes," she said, in the same glacial tones, "before it takes effect."

"You're mad at me—is it what I said about dead bodies?"

"That—and everything."

"What's everything?"

Doc struggled to an upright position. "I'll just never understand," she said. "Why? Why did you do it, Twinky?"

He backed up against the desk, standing bolt upright, like a prisoner hearing the charges against him.

"Well?"

"Well—I'm not like you, Doc."

"I see. It's my fault."

"Of course it's not your fault. It's just that you're . . . so damn capable. Everything comes easily to you. Medical school. The chief residency. Running a practice."

"You think it was easy? That's a laugh. Nothing came easily— because nothing!—ever does!—come easily! That's why you have to keep trying, keep working—and do whatever needs to be done." She glared at the desk.

He turned and saw the folder of material for his new campaign. "First thing tomorrow I'm going to work on it. I am, Doc—right after my run. And about that other business—I told you I'm sorry. I'm sorry, I'm sorry, I'm sorry. How many times do I have to apologize?"

"You'll never do it again?"

"I told you—never. And it was just the one time." He knelt by the bed. "Doc, my darling Doc." He stroked her hair back, off her forehead. "Our troubles are over."

"Then why were you looking in Zip's office?"

"I wanted to see if that damn bear was still in there."

"What if it is?"

"I'm afraid someone else will find out."

"You're such a wimp, Twinky." She looked scornfully at his nightshirt.

He looked down at the Superman emblazoned across the front. "It's just a joke."

"You're a joke. You panic when there's nothing to panic about. You give in without a whimper. *I* never give in." She pushed him away, lay down, and closed her eyes.

He stood looking at her for a few minutes, then went to the dresser and began rummaging through the drawers.

"Twinky!"

He jumped.

She looked like a demon, dark hair straggling over the pillow, fierce black circles under her eyes. "Where were you—that day on the trail—when we separated?" She glowered, as if she meant to drag the truth out of him, but beneath the fury was a note of entreaty.

"I told you. I went to watch a foursome putt it out at the fifth hole."

"Then why didn't they see you?"

"I stayed back so I wouldn't bother them. I told you that. Why don't you trust me? You were alone, too, but I never asked what you were doing?"

"I was running."

"Then why didn't you see . . . ?"

"I must have run right by Zip." She yawned. "I was trying to beat my last time."

"See—that's exactly what I mean. You're so competent—always focused on the main goal. Always dependable. Dependable Doc. No wonder everyone confides in you—friends, patients."

"That's another thing," she said. "Honestly, Twinky, I wish you'd stop making jokes about how you help me practice medicine. People are going to start believing I do tell you about my patients." She gave another yawn and sank back.

"Feeling better?"

"I'll pull through."

"You should take it easy. Just sleep in . . . we'll have breakfast together right after—"

She groaned. "I don't want breakfast."

"Whatever you want—right after my run." He couldn't repress a delighted chuckle.

"Twinky," she said drowsily. "What do you . . . have planned now? That medicine . . . soporific effect."

"Oh, come on, Doc. This place needs lightening up." He was at the closet, looking through her clothes. "Remember the spinning lady—the lady in white?"

"Twinky, you're too much." But she gave a weak, indulgent chuckle.

"See, I knew I'd get you to laugh. I just hope Bruce and Carlotta are out early. They promised."

"All right. But then . . . after breakfast . . ."

"I'll get right on that campaign."

Twinky found what he wanted and put it out for the morning. Then he went out on the lanai and stood looking down at the beach, thinking about Beth and Link.

"Remember, Doc," he said. "Remember our moonlight walks?"

No answer. She was breathing regularly—dead to the world.

Hand in hand, they strolled along the beach, watching the waves roll in. "Makes me think of *From Here to Eternity*," said Link. "Deborah Kerr and Burt Lancaster on the beach. Remember?"

"You mean, 'I never knew it could be like this'?"

"All right. A cliché, but maybe then it wasn't a cliché." He turned and looked at her. "Remember the waves, while Deborah and Burt—"

"There are quieter beaches," Beth said quickly. "For instance, Dover—'The sea is calm tonight. The tide is full, the moon lies fair/Upon the straits . . .'"

"Great poet, Matthew Arnold, but . . . it must be the English climate. Speaking geographically"—he took her in his arms—"as well as romantically"—and kissed her, finishing his sentence a good while later—"when it comes to beach scenes, I prefer *From Here to Eternity*."

They walked on. Beth looked up at the hotel, gleaming white in the darkness, like a great ship moving through the night. "You know," said Link, following her look, "I saw you before we actually met."

"At the airport?"

"In the hotel lobby—when you were checking in. You looked so—"

"Exhausted?"

"Exhausted was not the word I had in mind. *Beautiful* would work—or *enchanting*." Their eyes met and they stopped walking.

"This is not," said Beth, after some time had elapsed, "in the best tradition of detective stories—and we are detecting."

"What about Lord Peter and Harriet Vane?"

"Lots of talk—but very little action."

"We could pretend," said Link, gazing at her profile, "pretend there was action."

"But good detectives stick with the facts."

"Oh facts—I like fiction. Let's return to literature," said Link. "I'm Darcy—you're Elizabeth. . . . You are, aren't you?—and it's almost the last chapter."

"That *might* work. There's a good deal of blushing, and talking of love, and walking without knowing where they're going, but . . . I don't think they actually—"

"We'll revise. All good writers revise."

Much later he said, "Great game. I like it. How about I'm Ladislaw and you're Dorothea?"

"That's not till the end—and I'm not there yet."

But you will be soon, he thought, and then you'll start my book. And then—he put the thought out of his mind. "Pretend," he said, reaching for her. "Pretend that you *have* finished."

A security truck rattled up.

"You people all right?" It was Beth's friend of the night that Eleanor . . . How could she have forgotten, even for a moment?

"Hi," she said. "We're fine."

"Never better," said Link. "We have identified every constellation."

"I didn't realize it was so late," said Beth, looking at her watch. They left, Link mentally cursing the entire Royal security staff and all its trucks.

CHAPTER
25

The phone was ringing as Beth opened the door.

"Where in hell were you?" The unmistakable cigarette voice of the English department secretary.

"Hi, Dot. I was out for a walk."

"A walk? What time is it there anyway?"

"Let's see—almost 1:00 A.M. What are *you* doing up so early?"

"Tell you later. Where in hell were you?" Dot repeated. "Out with a guy, I hope?"

"How are things?" said Beth. "What's going on?"

"The usual. Everyone skulking around complaining about the weather and quoting whatsit—*King Lear.* Bunch of pantywaists."

"How is the weather?"

"Snow and more snow. They're predicting six inches tomorrow. What's it like there?"

"Oh, it's gorgeous, Dot. But I've been—" She stopped. If she even mentioned the murder, she knew exactly what Dot would say: for God's sake, I was only kidding! Remember the last time. You were almost a corpse yourself.

"Now don't tell me you've been feeling guilty, darling," Dot was saying. "It is your off quarter. Listen, have you met any cute guys?"

"Matter of fact, I have."

"I knew it! Who is he? Hope he has money."

"Well, he's a writer—very attractive."

"A writer! What kind?" Dot asked suspiciously. "Don't tell me he writes *literary criticism,*" lacing the words with contempt. "Who is he?"

Beth told her.

"Lincoln Lowenstein! Can you beat that! His books are swell—and so is he. I've seen his picture in those fancy watch ads."

"Is that why you called? To check up on my love life?"

"No, darling. I called because Porter's on a rampage."

"No more stolen library books, I trust?" said Beth, who knew the department chairman saw himself as the protector of Midwestern's collection.

"No stolen books. That's history. Porter's fit to be tied because some student—sneaky little twerp—who worked at the registrar's office was phonying up the grades for his friends. Porter's running around like a chicken with its head cut off—wants everyone to verify their grades from last quarter. So if I read them off, do you think you could put your famous memory to work?"

Beth said sure, and Dot began reading off names and grades. So weird, Beth thought, as she gave Dot confirmations, to be verifying grades in Hawaii, especially at the Royal, where money counted more than a grade-point average. "That's right," she said, "C minus," picturing the lackluster student who went with the grade. And they had finished.

"Thanks, darling. Gotta go. Have fun with your new guy!"

"Well . . . maybe."

"Something's bothering you," said Dot. "What is it—that FBI agent of yours?"

"I told you—he's not mine. But I *was* thinking about Gil."

"Forget him. Didn't you say he was away? There's lots of fish in the sea. Go for it, darling. I always did." She chuckled. "And I had plenty of fun. What's wrong with that?"

What was wrong with it? Beth thought later, after Dot had briefed her on department gossip. Of course she was crazy about Link—no, she meant Gil. But Gil was off on some assignment— hush-hush, couldn't say where, or even when he would return. And here, with Link, somehow Gil had slid into the background. Well, what's wrong with that, she asked herself. She tossed her clothes on a chair.

Nothing wrong, she thought, as she stepped into the shower. Nothing but the world's assumption that it's okay for men to play the field, but a woman has only one romance at a time. Assumptions. She was sick of them. They trapped you. Sig assumed he was too old—and gave up on himself. She herself had assumed Doc was a typical society matron—and for a time she had underestimated Doc. And what about her assumption about Link's books? Maybe she was wrong there too. Well, the hell with assumptions. How often did she meet someone like Link? Attractive, sense of humor, intelligent—someone she could really talk to. She reached for a towel, Dot's words echoing in her mind. *Go for it.* All right, Dot. Maybe I will. But now she was exhausted, her mind swirling . . . Link . . . murder . . . Get to bed.

The phone rang.

"Where the hell were you?" said Sig. "First your phone was busy. Then you disappeared."

"I was in the shower."

"Well, put something on and come up. Link and I are waiting. I've had a brainstorm."

CHAPTER
26

L ink's face lit up when he saw her. "Thank God you've arrived," he said. Beth, almost embarrassed to look at him, eased into the opposite corner of the sofa.

"Sig caught me right away," Link was saying, "but then he said he wouldn't tell me a thing till you got here."

"I wanted both of you to hear it together," said Sig, looking very pleased with himself. Then he almost leaped out of his chair. "I figured it out!" he said. "I figured it out! It's the one-million-pound supermarket plot! I wondered why Zip took *Gotham.*"

Slow down, they told Sig, and asked, what was all this?

"What you said about *Gotham,* Beth. It kept going through my mind. And then I remembered." He took a deep breath. "I ran into Gail this morning." He told them about the load of mail for Zip. "Newspapers, magazines—*Gotham*! It's perfect!"

Perfect for what, they asked.

"*Gotham* is famous for its outrageous personals. Another strange ad would blend right into the crowd." He looked at their puzzled faces. "All right. I'll backtrack. Last year, when I was in London, the tabloids were full of a story about a blackmail plot against a supermarket chain—Sainsburys. There were threats to contaminate the food in some of the shops unless Sainsburys paid a million pounds."

"I still don't—" Beth began.

"The blackmailer instructed Sainsburys to put in ad in a newspaper lonely hearts column to signal they'd pay off. Sainsburys did place the ad. I don't remember the exact words. They were told what to say—something like: 'To the man in my life. I need to phone you.' But I remember how the blackmailer told them to end it: 'If shy, write to Rebecca of Mablethorpe.'"

"Oh the English," said Link. "Even the criminals are poetic."

"Are you saying," Beth asked, "that the reunion people were using the personals to respond to Zip?"

"Yes! He must have found some way to tell them what to write without giving himself away. They wouldn't associate *Gotham* with Hawaii."

"Maybe Doc was looking to see if Twinky had an ad in there," said Beth. "Maybe she wondered if he had agreed to pay."

"You said the hairdresser read an ad out loud," said Link.

"Yes—and she must have stumbled on the one Doc was looking at."

"Did Doc seem interested?"

"Just the opposite. Now that I think about it, Doc almost went out of her way to look bored. But if she wasn't interested," said Beth, with growing excitement, "why was she reading the personals in the first place?"

"How about Suzy and Carlotta?"

"Just the same—bored stiff."

"You'd hardly expect them to say 'let me have a look at that' if they'd been placing personals to a blackmailer," said Link. "What did the ad say?"

She told them about the interesting single white male who enjoyed travel and vigorous outdoor activity.

"That sounds like Zip," said Link. "Having his private joke. Travel—that's Hawaii. Vigorous outdoor activity—tennis, of course. What was the rest?"

" 'Seeking a successful young woman, 42-24-35.' "

"Awesome!" said Link. "Rebecca of Mablethorpe would envy those measurements."

"That's why I remember them," said Beth. "But what do they mean?"

"Someone," said Sig, "has to go over all the ads in the back issues of *Gotham*. Beth, I'm assigning you."

"I accept," she said, holding back a smile. Sig, who had been so fearful, had become confident—involved. He made her think of an indifferent student suddenly turned on to Victorian literature.

"Here's what we have," said Link. "We know the focus of the blackmail. We have some good guesses about the secrets, and about how the victims signaled a payoff."

"Guesses," said Beth. "That's all we have to go on so far. We still have to prove we're right about Twinky and Burt. We still have to find out what's wrong about the lottery."

"So it's back to sleuthing tomorrow," said Link, with much more enthusiasm than he had shown earlier in the evening.

"Right," said Beth, "and no more assignments. We'll all take everyone—except I'll take *Gotham*—and Sig, remember the masseur."

"Yeah, okay," said Sig in mournful tones. His own surge of enthusiasm had apparently diminished. "But there's one thing we haven't talked about."

They asked him what it was.

"The murderer. Face it—we could be making trouble for our-selves."

"Oh why worry?" said Beth. "The blackmailer is dead. Who's left to kill?" Then she remembered her feeling of being watched at Zip's office, and at once dismissed it as all in her mind.

"I still say," Sig insisted, "if someone killed Zip because he knew a secret—what happens to us if we learn the same secret?"

"Did you read the Reverend Osumi this morning?" said Link.

Sig groaned. "Curiosity Batteries Two?"

"I happen to have his column with me."

"For a novel?" said Beth.

"For Sig." Link pulled a crumpled paper from his pocket. " 'The best advice for overcoming needless worry, anxiety, and fear is never cross your bridges until you come to them. So many people make themselves miserable worrying about something that never happens. So many people make themselves unhappy anticipating trouble that never comes.' "

"I'm going to start reading that column and quoting it at you," said Sig.

Link walked Beth back to her room. "How about offering me a nightcap?" he said.

Go for it, she thought—and fizzled out. "How about a rain check?" she said, never dreaming how prophetic her words would be.

CHAPTER
27

SUNDAY

The kitchen staff knew it was going to be a bad day when the pastry chef called to say he wouldn't be in because his dog had died. They flipped to see who would tell the executive chef.

The food and beverages manager knew it was going to be a bad day when he saw that no tables were available in any of the dining rooms until after eight.

The reservations manager knew it was going to be a bad day when he saw the travel writer alert on the new-arrivals sheet, and discovered the promised room was occupied by a couple whom only an act of God could induce to change.

The towels were late. They were running short of chairs and umbrellas. It's going to be a bad day, thought the beach manager.

She watched the joggers heading for the trail. If *she* had the choice, she would have stayed in bed.

For Peggy, the exercise stations were the best part of the jogging trail.

"Can we stop at the rings, Daddy?"

"Why not?"

They did the rings together, and ran on, stopping at Sit and Reach, and again at Touch Toes. Once a man in a truck smiled and waved at them. They ran on—soon they would be at Knee Bends. And then, as they passed the mussed-up place all jumbled with dead trees and vines, she saw something white and pretty. "Oh look, Daddy. No, down there—I think it's a wedding dress! Let's go see."

"I don't know. It's kind of wild—you'll get all scratched up."

"But the dress. I could use it for a costume." She turned on the look that always made him cave in.

"Okay," he said. "But I'll go first."

So rough here, it was hard to keep up. She saw Daddy trip over something—it was a flashlight, one of those big ones, like a lantern. But he kept going, stumbling through the branches. He was way ahead of her now, getting close to the dress. Why was he stopping? He turned around. His face looked . . . funny. "Now, Peggy"—why did he sound so scared?—*"I want you to go back."*

"But I want to see!"

"No! Turn around! That's right. *Now, go back up and wait for me."*

It was his no-deals, I-mean-business voice. She went.

He watched Peggy climb, waiting until she reached the trail. She stood at the edge, looking down at him. "Good! Just stay there!"

He turned back to the dress. Jesus—white halfway up and then —Christ!—like a red vest. He edged closer. Good God. It was a man. His face, dead white, his eyes, wide open, astonished. The neck—he couldn't pull his stare away from the gaping wound, blood frothing out, soaking the ruffles around the collar.

Peggy leaned way over, trying to see, but Daddy was blocking her view. She felt a little funny, as if she was going to be sick.

She heard running sounds from ahead.

A man and woman, turning the bend, came toward her. So glamorous, both of them. Maybe they were movie stars. The maid had said that sometimes stars stayed at the hotel. "Hi," said the man. "Waiting for someone?"

Up close, she could see how handsome he was, definitely a movie star. The sick feeling went away. "I'm waiting for my father."

"That dress." The woman looked where Peggy was pointing. "I know that dress. It's Doc's kaftan."

Daddy called out that they should stay where they were, but they didn't even listen. First the movie star, then the woman, going down more slowly.

Now the movie star was next to Daddy. "Oh, for chrissake, Twinky," she heard him say. "I know it's you. I can see your shoes. . . . One of our crazy friends, playing a joke," the movie star said to her father. Then he started talking to someone else. "Great idea, Twinky, but the white lady only appears at night. I knew you were going to pull something like this. How tasteless can you get? Did you have to pick the same spot where Zip—? What is that stuff? Tomato juice? Come on, you can get up now." She saw him pull at a sleeve. Then . . . nothing. No more talking.

She leaned over as far as she dared. The movie star was just standing there, staring down. "Oh Jesus," she heard him say. "The neck—don't look, Carlotta."

The sick feeling started to come back. What was happening?

Don't think about it, she told herself. Pretend it's a movie. Think about movie stars.

"What is it?" said the Carlotta woman. She was pushing in front of the movie star.

Her scream, Peggy thought, was so . . . weird—not short squeals like her friends at Halloween parties—more actressy, high and very, very long.

"It's not a trick! Oh God, it's not a trick!"

No—don't think about what she's looking at. Think about her voice. That was actressy, too, the way it kept going higher and higher—like a terrified woman in one of the late movies she was not allowed to watch.

"What's not a trick?" Another man had run up—old, glasses, definitely not a movie star.

The Carlotta woman was looking up at them. "Oh, Burt," she said. "It's Twinky . . . and he's . . . he's . . . I don't know what's happening. I thought it was a . . . What'll we do? We have to have Twinky—we've always had Twinky."

It's a movie, Peggy thought, when the terrified woman laughs and cries and talks, all at the same time.

"Could you take it easy?" She could tell Daddy was giving the Carlotta woman a disgusted look. "I have my little girl up there."

"Burt, stay up there with the girl," said the movie star. "Is Suzy coming? For God's sake, don't let her see—"

"Look," said Daddy, as if he had finally figured something out. "Someone has to go back. And someone has to stay here with . . ." His voice sounded funny, sort of trembly. "Make sure no one messes around with . . ."

"I'll stay," said the movie star.

"I'll go back and get Security." Then Daddy was up, grabbing her hand so tight it hurt. She didn't care. The horrible movie was over.

"Come on, Peggy. Let's see how fast we can run."

"Wait," said the one called Burt. "I'll go with you."

Still holding her father's hand, Peggy leaned over for one more look at the movie star. "You go, too, Carlotta," he was saying, as he scrootched down to look at something. "I'll wait here with—" Goodness, he sounded as if . . . Did movie stars upchuck?

"No!" said the Carlotta woman. "I'm staying with you and Twinky."

CHAPTER
28

SUNDAY THROUGH TUESDAY

The second murder was followed by a severe storm that began in the afternoon and continued to rage with no letup in sight, inevitable encore discussions of murder one, and panic. Now even recent arrivals knew that the Royal had been host to two murders. But the hordes of guests who wanted to check out were stymied. The optimists, who hoped the weather would improve, discovered that two conventions—Shriners and clowns—had filled every room on the island. The pessimists, more interested in prolonging their lives than their vacations, were informed that high winds and torrential rain had closed the airport.

Meanwhile, the weather had changed the whole atmosphere of the Royal. They had closed the tall shutters so you could no longer look out at the ocean. They had pulled the roof over the atrium so you could no longer look up at the stars. The lobby was so battened down that one old-timer said it felt like London during the Blitz. Outside, fierce winds howled and rain burst down in floods. Never, said the guests, as they followed the line of umbrellas to the dining rooms, never, even in Texas, had they seen rain like this.

The staff were driven wild with complaints. "Give me five more ways to tell them why the sun isn't out," said one of the beachboys. "They keep asking what I'm going to do about the rain," said the reservations manager. "They must think I can control the heavens." "I thought he was going to punch me out," said the golf starter, who had dragged a man off the windswept ninth hole. "I told him a tree could fall on him." "Doesn't it ever rain where they live?" said the bartender at the cocktail terrace, where business was brisk.

Confined to the hotel, the guests had developed a virulent Hawaiian cabin fever. The fitness room reported a slugging match over the StairMaster. The beauty salon reported a tantrum when one of their best clients could not get her husband an appointment for a pedicure and facial. The game room, in late afternoon, provided the only quiet moment of the day. Guests, waiting for the weather report, crowded in front of the hotel's one television, only to hear—"What can I say, folks? The weather is terrible. Now on to the rest of the news."

The weather loomed so large it almost took precedence over the murders.

But not for the trio of detectives. What surprised Beth most was Sig. From him she had expected fear, gloom—an I-told-you-so reaction. Instead, Sig was furious.

He was angry on behalf of the hotel—what business did this murderer have sending guests into a panic, tormenting Bucky, generating barbaric headlines: DOUBLE SLAUGHTER AT MOVIE STAR HAVEN,

ALOHA ASSASSIN CUTS LOOSE AGAIN. His peaceful retreat was being destroyed. It would end with the Royal reputed to be like that place —what was it?—the one with Legionnaires' disease.

He was angry that he had lost a friend. So what if Twinky was going to jump out of the bushes, flash a light on himself in the dress and scare the hell out of Bruce and Carlotta? Twinky was always out for a good time. That was what made him so lovable. Let's find the—the—let's find out who did it.

He was angry with the police. He had heard from Security that the police were looking for someone off the property—one of the construction workers, working on the main road. And why? Because they were shifty-looking; some of them, wore earrings. And because Twinky's Rolex was missing. Any fool could figure out the watch had been taken to throw the police off.

For Sig had bought Beth's theory completely—the murderer had to be one of the reunion group. Did he think the same person had committed both murders? Of that he was not sure—but same kind of wound, same kind of weapon—and where the hell was the weapon? Let's find it, he said.

As to other perplexing questions, Sig tossed them off, returning always to the reunion group.

Late Tuesday night they were in Sig's suite, the DO NOT DISTURB sign on the door, and Link was raising the question of why. Why kill Twinky when the blackmailer was dead? Easy, said Sig. Twinky knew someone's secret. I told you anyone who knew something was in trouble. Let's find out what Twinky knew.

What about how? Beth asked. Wouldn't it have to be someone strong, one of the men? Nonsense. Any of them could have done it. Sig had worked in an emergency room when he was in college, and he had seen plenty of slit throats. It didn't take any great technique or strength. The usual slice—right under the chin from ear to ear—worked fine, especially if you cut so deep you got the arteries. But you had to do it from behind. That was why it had to have been someone Twinky knew, someone who could get him way down off the trail, and then sneak in back of him.

Then didn't that narrow it down to Carlotta, Bruce, and Burt—the ones on the trail? No, said Sig. He refused to exclude Suzy. So what if she had been seen having coffee. Everyone knew she always met Burt right after and went with him on his second round. She had to have been somewhere nearby. He would not rule Doc out either. Security had told him that when the police came to her room, Doc had been in running clothes, sweaty. She had said she was going out to get some air—but she could have gone out earlier.

No getting around it—one of the group did it—and he was going to find out who. They all were. He himself was going for another massage. So what if the masseur's schedule was crowded. He hoped he still had some influence at this hotel. "And the two of you should get right on it too—everything we discussed—and more."

As to telling the police their theory, they were all opposed, Link because they had no proof. "We have enough guesses for a three-volume novel," he said. "But we've got nothing that titillates police—no fingerprints, no shreds of fabric, no hairs."

Beth wanted to wait for absolute certainty. "I cooked up this theory," she said, "and I feel responsible. I don't want to ruin reputations—not before I have proof. And what if I'm wrong? I think I'm right, but—"

"You're not wrong," said Sig. "And we can't stop now. If we bow out and let the police take over, there'll be another murder—I can feel it coming. And then what happens to the Royal?"

"Not to mention the victim," said Link.

"I keep seeing Twinky's face," said Beth. "I feel so guilty—as if I failed him."

"How could you have prevented it?" said Link. "As it is, it's going to be a wicked job to find out." He looked at the landscape, black with rain. "I don't know that we can."

"Did you see Osumi today?" said Sig. He reached for the paper. "It's called 'Do Something,'" he said, and began reading, a note of triumph in his voice. "'Someone said, "When I can't see any way out, I do something anyway." This is good advice to anyone who is in despair. . . . There is no use brooding over what has happened and indulging in self-pity. You may feel trapped but don't give up hope. With God's help, if you keep on trying, you can find a door that will get you out.'"

He stood, as if to give more import to what he was about to say. "First thing tomorrow, I'm going for a massage."

CHAPTER

29

WEDNESDAY

The storm and the frustrations continued unabated. The hotel rose to the challenge magnificently with around-the-clock movies, bridge tournaments, indoor aerobics, even an indoor golf clinic. In a letter signed *"Mahalo nui loa* for your understanding," management offered more activities—a back-of-the-house tour, an art tour, and on Thursday, rain—the gods forbid—or no rain, a Shipwrecked Cocktail Party, dress appropriate to disaster at sea.

Beth chose to ignore the morning's events. Rain lashing at her, wind whipping her umbrella inside out, she fought her way to the tennis courts. She looked through the window and there, seated at Zip's desk, was Gail. When she saw Beth, she leaped up and opened the door.

Suppressing her excitement at actually being inside Zip's domain, Beth mumbled excuses—felt so confined, just had to get out. Gail hardly noticed. She took Beth's raincoat, threw her some towels, and cleared off a chair. "God, am I glad to see you," she said. "The police finally finished in here, and I've been going through Zip's things. I hate it. Stay and talk."

It was more stay and listen, as Gail sang Zip's praises—so great to work with, never a mean word, not like some pros. Such a tragedy—he had such big plans—going to Wimbledon this year—paid a fortune for tickets—wouldn't tell me how much. Beth listened—and looked, trying not to appear overly inquisitive. The office was jammed with the usual detritus—rackets and covers piling up on the floor; kitschy tennis figurines cluttering the desk; tennis cartoons and photos of a smiling Zip, with Royal guests, covering the walls.

"Oh, you're looking at Zip's keepsake shelves," said Gail. "Those shelves! The one thing he was fussy about—always the same knickknacks, always in the same place. Things people sent him, he said. Brought back memories. Guess he was just a sentimental guy." She frowned. "Where's his Hubba Hubba Girl?"

"Hubba Hubba Girl?" said Beth.

"That's what Zip called her—really a Barbie doll, but someone had dressed her up 1940s style, right down to the platform shoes. She was always between the Ping-Pong balls and the teddy bear. What would the police want with a doll?"

"Quite a collection," said Beth. "Mind if I look through it?"

"Not a bit—nice to have company while I work," said Gail as she opened a drawer. She started tossing papers in the wastebasket.

Beth made a show of looking at the other things on the shelves, then picked up the teddy bear and looked at the menu—Gigio's Ristorante, San Francisco.

"Now why," said Gail, "would he save something like this?"

She handed Beth a faded scrap of paper. It was a clipping from an
advice column, a "Dear Abby" letter from a woman who was a
junior executive at a large firm. She had submitted what she
thought was a good idea to a vice president. The vice president
had shown so little enthusiasm that the woman assumed he was
not impressed with her suggestion. But the following week—

> he showed my idea to the president of the company as though
> he had originated it. The president thought it was brilliant. I am
> very resentful, seeing his career flourish and not my own. Any
> advice?

Let it go, was Abby's advice—"and the next time you get a
brilliant idea submit it to the president yourself."

Scrawled in the margin were some notes. "T? B? T *and* B."

"Is that Zip's writing?" said Beth.

"Yeah—what do you think it means?"

"I can't imagine." But she could, and her heart was beating
rapidly.

"What about the letter?" said Gail.

"The letter? I'm not thrilled with Abby's advice. How often do
you get a brilliant—"

"Yeah—I suppose so. But I mean, why would he save a thing
like that? And look—he made some copies. Probably had some
joke up his sleeve. Zip loved a good joke. I just hope the new pro
. . . Oh, well . . ." She tossed the clipping and copies away, and
continued looking through the drawer. After a fast glance to make
sure Gail was engrossed, Beth fished the clipping and all the copies out of the wastebasket.

"Well! Here you are, Hubba Hubba Girl," Gail said tenderly.
"Poor thing. All the way in the back. See how cute . . . now this
is really strange. I swear I never saw it before." She was studying

a yellow tag around the doll's neck. "What the heck was he thinking of?"

Beth read the tag. "Business closed due to untimely death in the family."

The writing was Zip's.

CHAPTER
30

"Yeah, massage is the number one way to relieve stress."

"Lots of stress this trip," said Sig, hoping for a reply to this, his third attempt to get a conversation going about the murders.

The soft music, added since his last visit, perhaps to drown out the howling winds. The dimly lit room. The masseur's skillful hands. Sig's eyes started to close. . . . Wait, keep alert, figure out the right approach. Oh hell—what's wrong with being direct? "Did you know Zip Heinz?" His voice rang out in the darkness.

He felt the masseur's hands stiffen.

"I gave him the occasional massage."

"Like him?"

"He was okay."

Sig waited for more, but more did not come. "Just okay?" he said.

"Let me put it this way. The secret of success in this business is total equanimity. So as I drive in—I have cruise control so I don't have to work my feet—I prepare mentally for the day. I think of who's on my schedule, and I meditate, try to conjure up a compassion for the human condition. I tell myself the physical is not who this person is. I don't know who this person is in the universal scheme—it's like a test."

Great, a philosopher. "I gather Zip was one of your tests. Did he come in without taking a shower?"

"Zip? Never. He was immaculate."

"Then what . . . ?"

"Oh, I guess you could say he was hostile."

Sig seized the chance. "Hostile? How so?"

"You've got a knot here. . . . Let me work it out."

What, Sig asked himself, made this guy turn into a clam since my last visit? Wonder if employees have been warned not to talk about the murders. Well—try a universal approach. "Do people talk very much when they get massages?"

The masseur poured on more oil. "Some do. Some don't."

"Do you encourage them to talk?"

"I don't encourage talk and I don't discourage it."

Maybe flattery. "Good thinking. Sounds like you wait for a cue. Not everyone would know to do that."

"A good therapist learns how to read clients," the masseur said complacently. "You learn to recognize the people who can't relax without talking. They use talk to let down the way some people use alcohol. Either way, once they relax, they let loose with the lip—sometimes they share information they don't mean to share."

Share? A social worker as well as a philosopher. "How about Zip? Was he the kind who relaxed by talking? Did he"—Sig winced mentally—"share?"

"I guess you could say that."

"What did he talk about?"

A moment's pause. "Mr. Winterfield, are you trying to pump me?"

"Yeah, I guess you could say that." Sig moved away from the working hands and sat up. "Look, what's your name?"

"Norman."

"Well, Norm—"

"Norman."

"Norman, I'd like to know your thoughts about Zip."

The masseur left the table and flicked some switches. The music died out, the light came on, and the massage studio turned into an ordinary, rather spartan, room. Sig wrapped himself in the towel and moved to the edge of the table. "Norman," he said, "I'm playing at being detective—got a bet on."

The masseur pulled a stool over to the table and seated himself opposite Sig. "Big stakes?" he said, looking at Sig intently.

Sig could read the thoughts that accompanied the masseur's changing expressions: this guy's a little nuts . . . what harm will it do . . . no work . . . maybe a bigger tip.

"I don't know that I can tell you that much," he said.

"Anything . . . anything at all, Norman. I want to win this bet."

"Big stakes," the masseur repeated, giving Sig a shrewd stare.

"The biggest."

For a time it was quiet. Then the masseur said, "It may sound funny, but I was one of the few people around here who wasn't crazy about Zip Heinz."

"Why is that?"

"I don't know—maybe because he bragged."

"Bragged about what?"

"Zip was an electronics whiz, so he was always bragging about things he could do with machines. I'm not into that, so I didn't pay much attention."

"What else did he brag about?"

"Oh, his clients, all his wonderful friends among the guests. But then he changed his tune."

"How do you mean 'changed'?"

"Let me put it this way. Someone who teaches tennis at a resort the way he does—did—could get bitter. You spend a lot of time hanging out with rich people. You get to thinking that you're the same as they are, that they're your friends. Maybe you are their friend, on a certain vacation level—but it's not the same."

"And Zip thought it was the same?"

"Let me put it this way. Zip had plenty of smarts, but when it came to financial things he asked his rich friends where to put his little bundle. Me, I know better. You've got to invest in what you know about. I'm putting my wad in a little company over on Maui—they make a great massage oil. It's going to be used all over; here, on the mainland. Give it some time and—"

"But what about Zip?"

"Yeah, Zip. Let me put it this way. The guests are always giving each other stock tips. But where do these tips come from? They come from one rich person who's heard something from another rich person. They're not real insider tips—and you're crazy if you invest, because these people don't know shit about the companies they're telling each other about."

"What does this have to do with Zip?"

"He got a few tips that he just followed blindly. Some worked out—some didn't. A few times he had some big losses."

"Was that all?"

"What I heard was that he got a tip from some people who told him it was a sure thing, on ice. Zip put everything he had in it, even went into hock. I don't know for sure, but I think he was in big to the Mafiosi. And he lost his shirt. That's when he turned hostile, got an attitude about the guests. To their faces he was their friend—but not to me. He started telling me things about his so-called friends—maybe because I'm sort of new here, don't have cronies to gossip with. So he used talking to me to get it out of his system, get even."

"Get even with who? The ones who told him about the sure thing?"

"Them probably, sure, but he was getting even with everyone —with all those filthy rich bastards who could afford a loss, or afford to wait it out until the market came back. He said to me once, 'What's a loss of fifty or a hundred thou to them? Their lives don't change.' So he trashed everyone. Mr. So-and-So is here with a swell chick—not his wife. Mrs. So-and-So was running around the beach topless last night—high as a kite. There's a bunch of so-and-sos who don't deserve their money—they got rich by cheating big."

"Did he ever say who got rich by cheating big—or how they cheated?"

"He never said who and he never said how. Don't know why —he wasn't bashful about naming the others."

"Any theories about who killed him?"

"I don't know who—the scuttlebutt is it was someone off the property. But I know why."

Sig felt a surge of hope. "Why?" he said. "Why was he killed?"

"I think he offended the spirits."

"You believe in the spirits?" said Sig. "Are you from around here?"

"I'm from Iowa. But when you're on an island, living with the constant threat of earthquakes, tidal waves, monsoons, volcano eruptions—you start believing in the spirits."

A soft knock on the door. The masseur looked at his watch. Sig got off the table and dressed quickly.

The masseur's face lit up like a torch at a luau. "Thank *you,* Mr. Winterfield! Come back soon—we can work on that knot in your neck."

CHAPTER
31

"Who gets the fruit and who gets the fruit with the champagne?"

The questioner was a woman Link had nicknamed the Boston Dragon. Her imperious manner, her high-necked print dress and sensible pumps combined in his mind to make her the epitome of an early-twentieth-century Boston matron. She carried a cane, which she used only for pointing, and she had been hectoring the guide since the tour had begun.

"The philosophy of the Royal," the guide had announced, "is to do whatever it takes to make a guest happy—and never rest on our laurels." Thus, he continued, they were constantly improving, redesigning the facilities, redecorating the rooms . . . "And you should get rid of those soft mattresses!" the Dragon said viciously. "I don't like soft mattresses!"

"When I first started working here," the guide said quickly, "I always used to come in through this entrance"—he gestured at the tall, imposing double doors—"but I could never find it to go back. That's because instead of the typical metal service entrance, the Royal has created an entrance that matches the beautiful wood and moldings elsewhere in the hotel. . . . And now"—he opened the doors—"for a look at what makes the hotel work, the part of the hotel that guests seldom see: the—uh—bowels of the building." The Dragon gave him a look of disgust.

The guide had taken them first to Room Service, where he showed off the service carts: "One thousand dollars per cart, two hundred dollars per wheel—noiseless so they won't disturb guests who are still asleep." The Dragon had sniffed disdainfully, clearly thinking that guests should be up and about early anyway. Then the guide pointed out the computer screen that showed the name and room number of the person calling in. "Last night," said the Dragon, "I ordered breakfast for six forty-five—now stop it, Lydia," she said to her daughter, who was pulling at her sleeve. "I'm going to have my say! They said they were booked for six forty-five and I'd have to wait until seven." The guide apologized profusely, and said he'd look into it.

When they reached the central kitchen, the guide had become euphoric: "glorious kitchen—you'd never see so much space in another hotel . . . extensive menus . . . the Raffia alone has thirty items."

"Well, I'm pleased to hear it," said the Dragon. "I thought you were cutting down. We've been eating in the main dining room all week and no one has offered us a dessert menu."

The guide looked as if he wanted to throw himself on top of the huge dishwashing machine and cry. "That's one of the reasons we have these tours," he said bravely, "to hear guests' comments. I'll look into it right away."

Now the Dragon was aiming her cane at the lineup of trays, some with fruit, some with fruit and champagne. "Get one of those envelopes, Lydia." Her daughter retreated. "Very well. I'll get one myself." She reached up with her cane, knocked an envelope to the floor, and told Lydia to pick it up. " 'Welcome to the Royal,' " she read. " 'We hope you enjoy your stay.' " Then she pointed her cane at the guide so fiercely that Link wondered if a concealed knife would suddenly flash out. "Exactly what our card said—but we only got the fruit," and she grilled the guide mercilessly until he finally admitted that the champagne and fruit combination went to guests who were longtime returns.

"We have been coming here for *years,*" said the Dragon, "and we only got the fruit." Murmurings of "we only got the fruit too," were heard, and some of the tour party looked accusingly at the guide. "It must be the rooms," said the Dragon. "That's it!" She glared at the guide. "The champagne goes to the ocean views, doesn't it?"

The guide evaded the issue, saying that if she would let him know her room number, he would have a deluxe tray sent up today.

The Dragon nodded haughtily.

Perfect, Link thought, she'll be perfect for the chief hospital executive. I'll make her a man—about fifty—he couldn't wait to get back to his room. He had the feeling that if he started taking notes here, the Dragon would confiscate them. Beth had told him he might dig up something useful on this tour. How right she was—but nothing to do with the murders.

In the pastry kitchen, the Dragon looked on contemptuously, while the rest of the party exclaimed over the trays of pies and cakes. One of the chefs stopped kneading dough and held out a tray of macadamia nut cookies. The other guests grabbed gleefully, but the Dragon refused. "I'm on a special diet. You never think about people on diets." The guide mumbled that on twenty-four hours' notice a guest could order any special diet item. "Well, why," said the Dragon, "didn't anyone tell us that? And why should it take twenty-four hours?"

Daughter and guide looked so miserable that Link felt he had to do something. "These are wonderful," he said, taking another cookie. "Do any of you ever eat them?" he asked the chefs. "Don't see how you can resist."

"Not us," said a chef. "To be honest, we get tired of them—but our tennis pro loved these cookies, used to come by early evenings and—" He stopped short after a look from the guide.

Just then something clicked in Link's mind. "What time do they make up the fruit and champagne trays?" he asked.

"Early evening," said the guide.

"When are they sent up?" He couldn't help sounding excited.

"Late morning," said the guide, and Link was jubilant. Beth had been right after all. Then, apparently thinking he had an insurrection on his hands, the guide said, "I'll see that all of you are sent deluxe trays tomorrow."

CHAPTER
32

The phone rang as Beth entered the salon, and the shampoo girl, drying her hands on a towel, ran to answer it. "No openings today. How about tomorrow at five-thirty? No, I'm sorry, we can't"—making a face at the telephone. "Do you want that 5:30?"

Beth waited at the desk. The salon was in a frenzy, the atmosphere as frantic as registration for fall classes. Manicurists rushed to get fresh water, hairdressers raced from one client to the next. It seemed as if every woman in the hotel had decided to comfort herself with beauty. Every chair was filled—women getting their eyelashes dyed, women with their hair wrapped in foil, women with their feet resting in sudsy water.

"Sorry, so sorry." The shampoo girl hung up, looking defeated. "Sorry," she told Beth. "We're full up. Try calling in later . . . maybe a cancellation—"

"Oh I'm not here for an appointment," said Beth, and the girl sank back in relief. "I wonder—do you have any old issues of *Gotham* I could see?"

"Ran out of reading material?" said one of the hairdressers sympathetically. "Take her to the storeroom, Donetta. We've got tons of stuff." Beth was ushered to a back room, where Donetta pointed to some cartons on the floor, said, "Take what you want, it doesn't matter," and rushed away.

Beth waded in. When she had finished, she had gleaned, from the stacks of fashion, hair, and decorating magazines, eight issues of *Gotham*. Enough for a start.

Now, where to go with her gains? The thought of her room was depressing. Too quiet. Even when she was doing research in the library, she liked the feel of people around her. Remembering a space she had discovered, she ran up to the fifth floor. She was in luck. The small lounge, tucked away in an alcove beyond the elevators, was empty. She settled in a comfortable rattan sofa and picked up the *Gotham*s.

The ads were tantalizing, a story in themselves. Everyone was searching for Mr. or Ms. Right and everyone knew what they wanted: "Seeking a worldly woman"; "Seeking an earthy, intellectual man"; "Seeking a witty, nonreligious Christian"; "Seeking an articulate Jewish beauty." Just one—desperate? open-minded? —sought only "a man."

Their personalities varied, but the seekers, one and all, were attractive: "Good-looking, hardworking vegetarian"; "Shapely, fun-loving birdwatcher"; "Slim, doe-eyed, Ivy-educated flute player"; "Sensitive, nonsmoking, Cary Grant–type, bored with urban women."

Beth tore herself away from the Cary Grant–type and started reading more seriously. At least a dozen single white males enjoyed travel, but of this group only four had a post office box in New Jersey, among them the ad she had heard in the salon. Now she read the ad in its entirety.

> Interesting, single white male. Tall, 6'4", enjoys travel and vigorous outdoor activity. Seeking intelligent, successful young woman, 42-24-35, who loves puppies. See photo in *New York Times*. Reply POB 718, Apple Tree, New Jersey.

A photo of puppies? Something went off in her mind. What was it? She turned to the next ad.

> Interesting, single white male. Height 5'10". Enjoys travel and vigorous outdoor activity. Seeking intelligent, successful young woman, 36-28-36, who likes Art Buchwald–type humor. See *New York Times*. Reply POB 718, Apple Tree, New Jersey.

Curious. The male remained interesting, but his height had changed. The woman remained voluptuous, but her measurements were different. And what was it about Art Buchwald? Think. She almost had it.

In the next ad, the interesting male omitted his height. Instead, he was "tall, muscular, 220 pounds," and he now sought a 38-28-35 woman for a "sharing Zelda and Scott relationship. See editorial, *San Francisco Examiner.*"

Beth stared ahead, thinking, vaguely aware of passersby slowing to look at her curiously. Once she felt someone looking at her, but instead of slowing the person hurried by. She looked up, but whoever it was had turned the corner. She shrugged and returned to the last ad.

Now the male was "tall, athletic, 34-inch waist." He was still seeking an interesting, successful young woman. Now, however, she measured 38-26-38, and she appreciated "brilliant ideas. See this week's 'Dear Abby' column."

"Dear Abby." At that moment she made the connection. The puppies—Art Buchwald—Zelda and Scott—they were one and the same. She had it now, and she saw that they had been looking at the ads from the wrong angle. Should she tell Sig and Link? No, she would keep it to herself for the time. She wanted to think some more about those changing numbers. She jotted down some notes, and as she did so, she felt a glow of satisfaction. They were moving forward fast now, she felt sure, faster perhaps than she realized.

CHAPTER
33

THURSDAY

Later Beth was to look back on the party as a turning point. At the time, however, it seemed that they had accomplished nothing. In the interest of efficiency, the three had decided to go their separate ways and Beth, the first to arrive at the promenade courtyard, saw that management's all-out effort had backfired.

The decorations—the inspiration, gossip had it, of a junior manager who was a shipwreck buff—were an unfortunate choice. Dominating the food stations were ice carvings of ocean liners with ill-starred histories—the *Andrea Doria* pastas with *Stockholm* sauces; the *Lusitania,* petite lobster tails in miniature lifeboats; the centerpiece was a listing *Titanic,* with vodka in cavities scooped out of an iceberg, and caviar molded into life preservers.

Inevitably the talk turned dismal—"been here through earth-quakes, airline strikes, new chefs—all kinds of disasters—never murder. . . . police bad enough . . . when the weather breaks reporters all over the place—worse than when we were here for the eclipse . . ." Beth listened to scraps of gloomy conversation and felt her own spirits droop.

The managers, doing their best to mingle, were faring poorly, for the guests, feeling bad-tempered and put-upon, were taking the opportunity to complain about everything, from the air-conditioning (too much, not enough) to the plumbing (too noisy) to the decor (why the new bedspread colors?). Even Bucky was taking it on the chin. Backed into a far corner, he was being harangued by a fierce-looking woman with a cane.

Few had bothered with costumes, and those who had, a sad mix of pirates and sea captains, seemed out of place. Suzy seemed to be in costume, but Beth wasn't sure who she was supposed to portray. She was wearing a torn shirt and skirt, and she was talking chummily with a young woman serving hors d'oeuvres. In profile, they were almost mirror images—same size, same build. Remembering her responsibilities, Beth joined them, and was introduced to "our friend, Keke—usually does our room in the morning, she's doing double duty tonight." Beth asked about Suzy's costume. "Burt and I are lovers, stranded on a desert island —except he wouldn't let me dress him up."

"Now, Suzy," said Burt. "She wanted to cut a fringe on my best pants!"

"Oh wait," said a woman as Keke started to move on. She helped herself from Keke's tray, and turned back to her friend. "I'm down to my last book—*Emma.* I suppose it's all right, but it's like all those other old-time novels where women never actually *do* anything except go to tea parties."

"Sounds like fun," said Suzy.

The woman gave her a superior look. "What kind of a life is

that?" she said. "Give me a Judith Krantz or a Lincoln Lowenstein, where women have careers."

"Oh, I like them too," said Suzy, but the woman had moved on. "I've got another good one," Suzy told Beth, "for our next book club—*The Prince and the Pauper.* By Mark Twain," she added. "But you're a professor—you know that. I wish I could get Burt to read it."

"Let's get the professor's opinion," said Burt. "Beth, do *you* think I'd like it?"

After waiting in vain for Suzy to ask why *her* opinion wasn't good enough, Beth said, "I'm sure you'd like it," her cold tone wasted on both of them. She would have liked to tell Link about the encounter, but he had drifted over (great pun, she could tell him) to the *Andrea Doria,* where he was talking with Bruce and Carlotta.

"Nice costumes," Link said, looking at Bruce's tuxedo and Carlotta's long, graceful gown. "They are costumes?"

"We're Colonel and Mrs. Astor," said Carlotta. "You know— the *Titanic.*"

"There's a problem," said Bruce. "The Colonel didn't make it."

"Because you sent me off in a lifeboat, while you stayed on deck. You're my *hero,* darling!" said Carlotta, and flung her arms around Bruce's neck.

Really throws herself into a part, Link thought. Mindful of his detective work, he tried desperately to think of a way to work "sharing" into the conversation. But he had paid a visit to the *Titanic,* and the vodka had muddled his brain. He made a stab at it. "I took too much pasta. Anyone want to *share?*" he asked, emphasizing the word as much as he dared, looking for any kind of response. Not a flicker. Bruce shook his head.

"How about you, Carlotta? It's really good—want to *share?*"

She gave him a strange look and said she was sure that Mrs. Astor did not eat pasta. "I *have* to stay in character," she added as if her life depended on it.

Sig, who had taken Burt aside at the *Lusitania,* was progressing no faster. After some maneuvering, he had turned the discussion to junior lawyers, but all he could get from Burt were diatribes about writing. "Young lawyers today can't write a decent sentence."

"They're pretty smart anyway, some of them," said Sig.

"They may be smart," said Burt, "but they can't write English."

"Some of them"—Sig watched Burt closely—"come up with good ideas."

"If they do," said Burt, "they don't know how to put them on paper. Can't even parse a sentence. Never heard of parsing."

Just then Beth saw Doc come in. Looking haggard, she stood alone at the edge of the courtyard. Beth went over to talk to her, and asked how she was feeling. "I'm tired, Beth, tired of the police, tired of the hotel—I can't take it here without Twinky. I just want to go home. Sorry—don't mean to burden you—let's talk about something else."

So they did talk for a time, about the weather, about travel. And then, feeling like a traitor, Beth said she was thinking of a trip to San Francisco. "Someone was telling me about good restaurants. Ever hear of Gigio's Ristorante?"

"Gigio's?" Doc looked surprised. "That was a favorite of Twinky's."

"I'm sorry," said Beth. "I didn't—"

"It's all right—you couldn't have known. He used to meet clients there. It's a good place. Nothing fancy. Plain Italian food. Candles in wine bottles. Checkered tablecloths. They wrote all

over the tablecloth when they were presenting the big campaign.
. . . Hi, guys," she called to Suzy, Burt, Bruce, and Carlotta.
"Some reunion we're having," she said bravely.

Carlotta rushed to Doc's side and kissed her. Bruce put an arm
around her. Suzy and Burt stood stock-still, looking sympathetic
but awkward.

"Is it bent?" said Link. He was talking to the tour guide, who, it
came out, was an assistant manager.

"Is what bent?"

"Your ear. I thought it might be after that tour."

The manager laughed. "We're used to that kind of thing. Anyway, guests like that really care about the Royal. They think of it
as their place—and see it as their job to keep us up to the mark."

With little hope of learning anything useful, Link asked about
guests who kept coming back.

"It's interesting," said the manager. "After a few years, they
develop a routine. We even joke about it. You know it's one P.M.
when you see Mr. A. at the beach bar. You know it's six-thirty
P.M. when you see Mr. B. coming off the tennis courts. You know
it's ten P.M. when Mrs. C. goes up to put her jewels in the safe.
We used to say, 'You know it's six forty-five A.M. when you see
Zip coming off the trail—' " He broke off. "Shouldn't be talking
about that."

"Oh, what harm can it do? Did he really come off the trail at
the same time every day?"

"Every day, six forty-five, like clockwork. Then last year there
was some scare—Mr. Breneman thought he had a heart attack.
Doc—Mrs. Delorio—examined him and it wasn't anything. But it
got Zip worried about his heart. So he talked to Doc—Mrs.
Delorio—about running, and she told him he should take more
time for a cooldown, walk the last quarter mile. Told him if some-

one—even someone in good condition—just stops abruptly, the heart could get out of rhythm—fibrillate, I think she said. So after that Zip did an extralong slow down, and then we said—used to say—'You know it's seven A.M. when you see Zip leaving the trail.' "

The courtyard was abuzz with talk and laughter. One of the pirates was dancing a hornpipe to cheers and bursts of applause. The food and drink had taken effect, the gloom had lifted, the party at last was doing the work that had been planned for it. The staff started to relax and enjoy themselves. Across the courtyard, Bucky shook hands with the Dragon. "That was very interesting," he said. "Be sure to let me know if there is anything I can do for you. Anything at all," he said, taking a few neat backsteps to the elevator. The doors opened, and he disappeared.

The party continued without him, growing louder and louder. There was talk of leaving for dinner, other talk of who could be hungry now.

Then suddenly it was quiet. Everyone was looking at the stairway that connected with the lobby above. A small boy, hair wet and plastered down, was racing down the steps. He had something gold in his hand, and he was waving it triumphantly. "I found it! I found it!"

"What did you find, Bobby?" asked a woman, presumably his mother.

"The Rolex! It was in the Buddha. They told me it was good luck if I rubbed his belly and then put flowers in his lap. And I did it. I rubbed his belly, and put in some flowers—and it was there under some other flowers."

"Was that all you found?" someone said.

"What do you mean?"

"Was there anything else in the Buddha's lap?"

"Just the watch. Look at it, Mom."

A manager went over and talked to the boy, and after a few *but I found it*s he reluctantly gave up the watch.

The silence grew so deep you could almost hear the unspoken thoughts. The Rolex could mean that the murderer was not someone off the property. The Rolex could mean that the murderer and the weapon were still in the hotel.

In a few minutes, the courtyard was empty.

CHAPTER
34

"Do you think there was anything symbolic about hiding the watch in the Buddha?" said Link.

"I doubt it," said Beth. "Just a good way to dispose of it. Run up the stairs, drop the watch—and get out of there before you're spotted. Whoever it was could have done it just before the party, when most of the staff were down in the courtyard."

"Why not get rid of the weapon then too?" said Link.

"Maybe," said Sig, "someone still has a use for it."

Outside it was so dark that Sig had turned on all the lights in his suite. Beth looked at the rain, splashing on the lanai, overflowing the gutters. She felt gloomy, as if she knew something, something that would not surface no matter how hard she thought, as if when she did know, she would feel more depressed than elated.

"Come on, Beth. We need to talk," said Sig. His Hitchcock face alight with excitement, he looked completely different from the man who had pronounced himself too old for adventures. Link, next to him on the sofa, looked eager too. She couldn't help thinking how skeptical they had been when she first presented her idea, how she had worked to sell them. Now they were believers and ready to go, while she . . . she was afraid of what she had set in motion. Enough. She walked away from the glass doors and sat facing them. "Let's talk about Zip," she said. "What have we found out?"

"Zip," Sig began enthusiastically, "was a very angry man who needed money in a bigger way than we thought."

"The couple who gave him the sure thing," Link said when Sig had finished. "That would have to be Bruce and Carlotta—the tip that went sour. Too bad Zip never told the masseur who the so-and-sos were who got rich by cheating big."

"We know he meant Bruce and Carlotta," said Beth. "And we know now that he was angry at the whole bunch—even vengeful. He had a cruel twist." She told them about the Hubba Hubba Girl and the note around the doll's neck. "Poor Eleanor. I'm certain now that Zip was outside her room—probably put a note under the door."

"I still say he couldn't have gotten away with that method forever," said Sig.

"He didn't," said Link. "He had another way to blackmail the others."

"You know—and you haven't told us?" said Beth.

"Just waiting for the right moment. I will now relate the Tale of the Tour, otherwise known as the Fruit and Champagne Wars." He made a good story of it, acting out the relentless Dragon and the vanquished manager. . . . "And when the Dragon knocked the envelope down I saw it wasn't sealed. Zip could have inserted his own note in the envelopes. It would have been easy for him to slip in and out—the trays can't be seen from the pastry kitchen."

"Great, Link!" said Beth, catching his enthusiasm. She liked the teamwork, and the feeling that the puzzle pieces were gradually coming together.

"We still don't know how he blackmailed outside the hotel," said Sig.

"I think I know," said Beth.

"She knows," said Sig, "and she didn't tell us. Come on, Beth, give!"

"Through *Gotham*!" she announced.

Sig, sounding hurt, said but that was the victims responding to Zip.

"You put us on the right track, Sig, but we were assuming a repeat of what happened in England. In this case it was the blackmailer—Zip—using the personals to send messages to his victims. Take a look."

After they had scanned the personals, they asked how she knew they were all from Zip. All of them, she pointed out, gave the same post office box in New Jersey. "He rented an address they'd never connect with Hawaii. And they all start with the same single white male. What's significant are the way his measurements change—from 6'4", to 5'10", to 220 pounds, to a 34-inch waist. . . . Don't you see?" They looked blank. "They're deadlines—June fourth, May tenth, February twentieth, March fourth."

"Nice work, Beth," said Link. "What do the women's measurements mean?"

"I'm not sure."

"Let me see them again," said Sig, putting on his glasses. He shoved aside a vase of flowers and spread the magazines over the table. After a few minutes he said, "They could represent the money they were supposed to send. If you add up the numbers as single digits—4+2+2+4+3+5—you get 20. Add up the others and you get 28, 29, and 30. Then add a few zeroes, say four, and you get 200,000, 280,000, 290,000 and 300,000. Could have been three zeroes, but more likely four—I'm sure he thought his victims had unlimited cash flow."

They congratulated Sig, who looked pleased and said anyone would have thought of it. "And I don't have a clue about the messages."

"That's what's most interesting," said Beth. She showed them the 'Dear Abby' letter.

"Okay," said Sig. "Someone had an idea stolen and wrote to 'Dear Abby.' That would certainly be a nudge the blackmailer could use. But Buchwald? Puppies? 'A sharing Zelda and Scott relationship'?"

"More nudges," said Beth. "All about idea-stealing—I remember reading about them. Art Buchwald sued Paramount for basing *Coming to America* on a script he wrote—and he won! The puppies has to be Jeff Koons and his 'String of Puppies' sculptures, which he sold for thousands. Fine—except the sculptures were copies of a greeting card photograph Koons had used without permission. The photographer sued, and the court—good judgment!—ruled that Koons had committed copyright infringement. As for Zelda and Scott—"

"No lawsuit," said Link, "but exactly the same point."

"Would someone enlighten me?" said Sig.

"When Zelda Fitzgerald's collected writings were published," said Beth, "it came out that Scott stole material—line for line—from Zelda and used it in some of his best-known novels. Without giving her credit, of course."

" 'Kid, you said it,' " Link sang. " 'They all forget they know you when it comes to credit.' "

"Your source?" said Sig. "Beth demands sources."

"Funny Girl," said Link. "And I have a funny idea that Zelda and Scott—the sharing relationship—were meant for Bruce. Remember, Beth, when you told us about Zip's 'share the glory' remark? Suppose you were right about Bruce, that he did use someone else's crazy system, and that by sheer good luck he came up with a winner. Suppose that Zip meant another kind of failure to share. People are always teaming up for the lottery. Suppose Bruce and this systems person had promised to share the winnings—and Bruce didn't keep his part of the bargain. If that came out—well, can you imagine Bruce and Carlotta without money? Or with only half their money?"

"Why didn't the other person lodge a complaint?" said Sig.

"Good question," said Link. "Guess we'll have to hold that one aside. I tried out the sharing on Bruce and Carlotta at the party—didn't get anywhere. I wish we had confirmation for someone."

"We do," said Beth. "From Gigio's Ristorante." She began telling them about her talk with Doc. . . . "And then Doc said that *they* wrote all over the tablecloth when *they* were presenting the big campaign. That's a complete contradiction of what Twinky told that kid at the tennis courts. 'I made the presentation,' he said. 'I wrote all over the tablecloth.' Pretty good confirmation that Twinky didn't come up with the idea on his own—especially when you add that to his ignorance about Teddy Roosevelt."

"Did you get anything else from the party?" Link asked.

"Not much. I talked to Suzy, but she didn't say anything revealing. Just talked about books. By the way, Link . . ." She told him about the woman who had praised his books. "Because your women *do* something," said Beth, "I've got to start your book!"

"Stick with *Middlemarch*," said Link, and asked Sig what he had learned at the party.

"I tried talking to Burt about getting ideas from juniors, but he was evasive—said they couldn't write well enough to put ideas on paper."

"Maybe that's the clue," said Beth. "Maybe someone told him an idea and he wrote it up and took the credit."

"We've been talking about *whys*," said Sig. "But we need to talk about *who*. Even if we leave some questions unanswered, we need to get down to *who* before . . . something else happens."

Beth sighed. It was the *who* that worried her. The puzzle part, unraveling the secrets, decoding the personals, had been fun, but this part, the *who*, was not fun. She got up and looked outside. Sheets of rain blotted out the grounds, blackened the sky and the ocean.

"Let's order drinks," said Sig.

"But it's only eleven," said Beth.

"I don't care. I can't stand one more minute of drear."

"Is that a word?" said Link.

"Drear, dreariness—whatever. We need to cheer up—get the old imagination going. Let's have a cerebral cocktail party." Sig went to the phone. "What'll you have? And please don't say orange juice."

Room service arrived with a tray of gin and tonics and a platter of canapés—shrimp, smoked salmon, papaya and prosciutto.

"Looks wonderful," said Sig. "You two working together?" he asked the women who had brought the order.

They giggled. "Manager said we should go in pairs today."

"But why? Oh, I see."

"Makes it slow," said one woman. "Lots of drink orders this morn—" She stopped, her eyes on the bathroom door, slowly opening. . . . She screamed just as Link came out.

"Want me to go back in?" he said.

"Sorry. We're all scared to death—everyone's scared, staying in their rooms."

By mutual agreement they abandoned all talk of the murders for thirty minutes. They drank, they ate the canapés. Link told war stories about publishing, Sig told them about his first court cases. Beth told them about a professor who had charged into her library seminar room, yelling at her students to shut up, because her discussion group was interfering with his research. Then Sig looked at his watch. "Let's go back to the first murder."

"That reminds me," said Link. "Zip had a routine." And he told them about his talk with the assistant manager. "What we need to find out," he said, "is who in the group—other than Doc, of course—knew about the cooldown."

"They all had to know," said Sig. "If the hotel staff knew, I guarantee it was common knowledge that Zip did a long cooldown before he came off the trail."

"The question is," said Link, "who had the opportunity?"

"Beth," said Sig, "you were out there and you haven't said a word."

"Yes." She shuddered. "I was out there." The events of that morning stood out as if they had happened an hour ago.

"Well? You must have seen Bruce and Carlotta—they're always first ones out."

"They were on the trail."

"So they had the opportunity."

"I suppose so."

"How about Twinky and Doc?" said Link.

"I saw them, after—I remember thinking they looked as if they'd been running, but I could have been wrong."

"Did you see Suzy?" said Sig.

"I saw her getting coffee—before I went on the trail. She couldn't have had time."

"You don't know how long she spent over coffee," said Sig. "She could have finished quickly and then run out there. What about Burt?"

"I saw him in the fitness room, pedaling on the bicycle—so that rules him out."

"Why are you defending everyone?" said Sig. "You don't know how long he pedaled—he could have gone out there. They all had the opportunity, same as with the second murder."

Not the second murder, Beth thought. Twinky. "Remember the old aloha spirit, take life easy" Twinky—lying there with his throat cut.

"But the second murder," Link was saying, "was different. How could the murderer know Twinky would be alone?"

"Everyone knew Doc was feeling lousy," said Sig. "It would have been a good guess that Twinky would be running alone."

"So," said Link, "they all could have done it—including Doc."

"Doc!" said Beth. "Why on earth . . . ?"

"Suppose that Doc, unbeknownst to Twinky, intercepted Zip's note, found out about Twinky, and then decided she didn't want to be tied to someone who would disgrace her in front of the entire world. It could rub off on her career."

"Pretty far-fetched," said Sig. "She'd kill her husband because he could make her look bad? Hey, she's not running for office. More likely, if she killed anyone, it was Zip."

"Okay, I've got a better one," said Link. "She killed Twinky because she was having an affair."

"An affair?" said Beth and Sig together.

"With Zip—and she thought Twinky killed Zip. Or maybe she was having an affair with Bruce, and she thought that Zip . . ." He looked at their faces and trailed off, grinning. "Sig, you said we should get our imaginations going. We've got to consider every possibility—no matter how remote."

"That's what comes of gin and tonics," said Sig, "or of being a novelist. Still, I don't think we can rule anyone out."

That was the problem. It could have been any of them—any of the friends she had made. But these friends, Beth reminded herself, were not what they seemed. Their reputations, some of them, were based on illusion—no, not illusion, on cheating big—and a form of cheating she despised. Cheaters, or partners in cheating—all of them. A murderer—one of them. And she had come to like them.

Friendly, blundering Suzy; good, dependable Doc; Burt, sexist, but lovable really with his silly, labored analogies. Bruce and Carlotta, show-offs, but with a wonderful zest for life. Good friends, long before she knew them. Who among them was capable of planning so deviously, murdering so cruelly? One of them was—she had to accept it.

"If we only had more to go on," Link was saying.

"Like what?" said Sig.

"I don't know—something private. We see their public faces. What are these people like when they're alone? If only there was some way to observe them, when we're not with them."

"Two-way glass?" Beth suggested.

"There's always the guest histories," said Sig.

"What's that?" said Link.

"Forget it—I'm joking."

"You're onto something. Come on, Sig."

"The hotel keeps files on guests that go back for years—they're all in the computer now."

"What kind of information goes into the files?" said Beth, interested despite her qualms.

"Oh, anniversaries, birthdays, room preferences, special diets—kinky things too. I heard they record it if you're here with someone other than your spouse—they make some note like 'Don't call her Mrs. She's not his wife.' "

"Sig," said Link, "you've got to get us into that computer."

"No. And again no. There are limits. I have a certain loyalty to the Royal."

It took another gin and tonic and at least thirty minutes of serious pleading before Sig threw up his hands. "All right, all right. I'm not making any promises, but I'll see what I can do. You know there are laws against this. So if I do get you to a computer —include me out. For this one, you two are on your own."

CHAPTER
35

FRIDAY, EARLY AFTERNOON

Tucked away behind the Royal's activity desk was the concierge's office, where the concierge was talking excitedly on the phone. "Isn't that very advanced? I thought they didn't roll over until—just a minute. Come in," he called. The door opened. "Well, aloha, Mr. Winterfield!"

"Aloha, Dennis!" They shook hands.

"I'll be finished in a second," said Dennis, returning to the phone. "Talk to you later—call me right away if she does it again." He hung up and smiled at Sig.

"How's Emily?" Sig asked.

"Wonderful! We have a baby—a daughter."

"Congratulations, Dennis!" Sig reached into his pocket. "Have a cigar! A baby—it doesn't seem possible. I remember when you were a kid at the front desk. What's her name?"

He told him.

"Spell it," said Sig.

"K-I-M-B-A-L-L-E."

"Kimballe. Very pretty. Say, Dennis, can you do me a favor and pull up my record? I want to see when I was here in '90. Can't remember if I was here at my usual time or in the fall."

"Of course, Mr. Winterfield." He turned to the computer, punched a few buttons and looked at the screen. "In 1990 you were here from February fourth to February twenty-fifth."

"Say, that's interesting the way you can get all the information. Can I see that?"

Dennis hesitated, ran his eyes over the screen, then said, "Sure. Take a look."

Sig leaned over. "SR," he said. "What's that?"

"Suite request."

"And AG—what does that mean?"

"Advise general manager of arrival."

"So Bucky is on the alert for me! And what's VP? Vice President?"

"No." Dennis smiled. "That means VIP guest."

"I'm flattered," said Sig, watching the screen go dark. "These computers are wonderful, but they're so complicated. How do you know what buttons to punch?"

"Nothing to it. Just my initials—and a five-digit password."

"Sounds like a spy story."

Dennis laughed. "Hadn't thought of it that way."

"Do you always use the same password?"

"No, Bucky's strict about that. We change our passwords every few months."

"Mr. Halloran." The girl from the front desk leaned her head around the door. "Can I see you a minute?"

Dennis excused himself. Sig looked around, saw Dennis still talking to the girl. He reached for a paper that he had seen Dennis use—saw it was a list of abbreviations—and tucked it under his aloha shirt.

When Dennis came back, Sig was looking at the photographs on the desk. "Oh, they're old," said Dennis, pulling out a hanging file of snapshots. Bravely, Sig looked at each. "What a smile! She looks like you. Oh cute, with the sunglasses." Then he thanked Dennis, gave his best to the family. At the door he turned. "Just remembered something. I have a friend here—Mr. Lowenstein."

"The writer! He's on our VIP list too."

"He's got a problem with his computer. I wonder—can he use yours?" said Sig, conscious of the paper under his shirt.

"Is he working on another novel?"

"Yeah. He has some kind of deadline. Let's see. . . . I don't know about these things. I think he said he has his disk, and that it would work with almost any computer."

Dennis ran a hand through his neatly combed blond hair, much like Bucky's. "Gee, Mr. Winterfield, I'd like to, especially with the novel and all, but his disc could implant a virus in the system." He looked embarrassed. "Please tell him I'm sorry, but it's the rules."

"Don't give it another thought," said Sig, cursing inwardly. "Thanks, Dennis. Aloha—and may the weather break."

"You said it," Dennis responded fervently.

Sig left, mulling over the possibilities.

LATE AFTERNOON

At the front desk, Sig had just delivered the punch line.

Jimmy roared. " 'There are skid marks in front of the cat!' Great, Mr. Winterfield. Did you hear the one about the doctor and the plumber?"

"No," Sig lied. They went on exchanging stories, trying to top each other, until Sig lowered his voice and said, "Jimmy, my boy, can you do an old man another favor?"

Beth looked at the time—after midnight. In less than an hour, Link would meet her. Would they come any closer to who . . . ? She thought again of *The Moonstone,* again remembering the character who had used *Robinson Crusoe* as his infallible remedy. When his spirits were low—*Robinson Crusoe.* When he wanted advice—*Robinson Crusoe.* On the table next to her lay *Middlemarch.* What would happen if she merely . . . She picked up the book. Trying to be casual, random, she flipped it open and her eyes lit on:

"How very ugly Mr. Casaubon is!"

"Celia! He is one of the most distinguished-looking men I ever saw. He is remarkably like the portrait of Locke. He has the same deep eye-sockets."

"Had Locke those two white moles with hairs on them?"

She laughed to herself—should she check for moles? Try again. Open it at a different spot:

In an instant Will was close to her and had his arms round her, but she drew her head back and held his away gently that she might go on speaking, her large tear-filled eyes looking at his very simply, while she said in a sobbing childlike way, "We could live on my own fortune—it is too much—seven hundred a year—I want so little—no new clothes—and I will learn what everything costs."

She chuckled. Did this mean Carlotta? One more try. She flipped to the middle:

In watching effects, if only of an electric battery, it is often
necessary to change our place and examine a particular mixture
or group at some distance from the point where the movement
we are interested in was set up.

Group—uncanny. And *distance*—well, why not? Why not think
back to the time before the murder, when everything had been
happy.

She saw Bruce and Carlotta zooming down to the tennis courts
—"Well, a-lo-*hah*!" She saw Twinky, pounding the dinner table—
"It's apple juice!" She heard Suzy, lifting her voice over the dryer
—"Oh, the speeches! Taxes this! Taxes that!" She heard Doc—
"Amazing what some women tell me about problems they've had
for years." Conversations, images, flooded back. She relived the
first days, remembering more and more. Then she let her mind
move beyond the murders. . . . Was it possible she had the answer?

There was a tap at the door.

CHAPTER
36

"You seem different," Link said as they walked down the atrium corridor.

"Different? Watch it!"

Three floors below, a security guard scanned his light over the doorways. They retreated to a lounge area, and watched the light move back and forth.

"What'll we say if he stops us?" Beth whispered.

"That we're on a midnight art tour," said Link. He tweaked the nose of one of the bronze Thai dogs guarding the lounge. "No law against taking a late stroll."

They waited until the guard's light disappeared, then moved to the opposite end of the corridor.

"Different how?" said Beth, as they went down the stairs.

"I don't know." He gave her a long look. "Same beautiful face, but it looks as if it knows something it didn't know before."

They reached a landing. "I do know something."

"What?" He put a hand on her arm. Another guard, just one floor below. They drew back into the shadows. He was coming closer. They pulled back a few more steps—Beth hit something that triggered a jingling. Oh God—she had backed into the bell collection. Wind chimes and temple bells were ringing softly. The guard looked up and moved toward the stairs. Then a gust of wind set everything clanging, even the elephant bells. He shook his head and turned back.

When he had been out of sight for some time, they continued downward. "Well?" Link whispered.

"I think I know who—but I'm not certain."

"You know who?" He forgot to whisper. *Tell me.*

"No, not until I'm sure. It wouldn't be fair."

"Fairness at this point? That's crazy. You're being like Dorothea."

Link was doing it, too, Beth thought, connecting everything with *Middlemarch.* "What do you mean 'like Dorothea'?" she said.

"Excessively conscientious, willful. Think of the disaster she brought on herself when—"

"Shhh." They had reached the side hall off the lobby. The lobby itself was deserted, a lone clerk at the desk.

"Let's make a run for it," said Link. "He won't see us."

"Wait," Beth whispered, her eyes on the clerk. He was standing. They watched as he walked away from the desk toward the back offices. He disappeared.

"Now," said Link.

"No!" Beth whispered urgently, nodding her head toward the stairway. A white figure came into sight—Doc! wearing sweats and running shoes, moving down the stairs like a sleepwalker.

"Quick!" said Beth. They backed into the ladies' room, left the door open a crack, so there would be no warning click. They peered out, saw Doc leave the stairs. She turned. She must have seen them, Beth thought. But then Doc veered away, crossed the lobby, and went down the stairs to the courtyard.

"Where could she be going?" Beth said softly.

"Running?"

"In this torrent? Maybe we should go after her."

"No time," said Link. "The clerk will be back any second. Come on!" They raced across the tile to the concierge's office.

A few minutes went by. The clerk returned to the desk. As he turned to reach for something behind him, someone swiftly crossed the lobby, moved back of a large Japanese screen, and stood motionless, eyes on the concierge's office.

There had been no trouble getting in. The door was open just as Sig had said it would be. Now, with the curtains drawn so the one dim light could not be seen, the office had become intimate, cut off from outside. To Beth it seemed as if they were down below on a ship. The only two passengers left.

Link was already at the computer. She pulled up a chair next to him. He pushed some buttons and the screen lit up. Muttering to himself, he pushed more buttons, swore softly.

"What's the problem?"

"It's asking for an access code—Sig said initials and a five-digit password. Thought he'd pick the usual, something easy to re-member, but DH-DENNY isn't working." He fiddled with DENHA, then HALLO, then LORAN. Nothing.

"How about Emily?" said Beth. "Sig mentioned that's his wife."

EMILY didn't work and neither did EMMIE. Nor did ROYAL or ALOHA or MAUNA (mountain) or MOANA (ocean). Beth looked around, saw the photographs. "The baby!"

"What baby?"

"He's got a new baby—that has to be it."

But she had no idea of the baby's name.

"Let's call Sig," said Link.

"We can't phone from here!"

"What choice do we have? Make it fast, though," he said as Beth picked up the phone.

"Quick, Sig. What's the baby's name? . . . Dennis's . . . Never mind why . . . What? . . . Are you sure? . . . Spell it. . . . Okay, I've got it. . . . Can't talk. . . . No one saw us. Stop worrying."

"Well?" said Link. She told him. "Jesus—how do we get five letters out of that?"

"Try KIMBA." They tried it. And KIMBY. And KIMMY. They tried one more. The computer moved into action and offered a menu. "Kimmi," Link said mournfully. "Forever doomed to daintiness. Let me see that sheet Sig gave us . . . Y for guest history." He punched a button. "Who first?"

"Let's try the Howards," said Beth.

He brought up Bruce and Carlotta, punched C for display guest history, and they learned that the Howards had been coming to the Royal for ten years, that after the first year they always stayed in the same ocean-view suite on the top floor.

"This doesn't tell us anything," said Link. "Why are we doing this?"

"Because I need to know more about *how*," said Beth. She looked at the sheet. "Try CMD for comments."

Prefer king-size bed.
Play Cole Porter—first day—terrace.
Provide extra hangers.
Provide cart for clothes.
Complaint—wants same bedspread colors—Mrs. Howard.
Complaint—wants same pictures—Mrs. Howard.
Complaint—breakfast cold—Mrs. Howard.
$$$$ beauty salon—Mrs. Howard.

$$$$ gift shop—Mrs. Howard.

$$$$ dress shop—Mrs. Howard.

Complaint—birds too noisy—Mrs. Howard.

Complaint—gift shop should carry better brands of cosmetics—Mrs. Howard.

CB CH

Complaint—gift shop should carry *Gotham*—Mr. Howard.

Complaint—unable to get desired reservation in Raffia Room—Mrs. Howard.

Complaint—slow service in the main dining room—Mrs. Howard.

Complaint—too cold in the Islands Room—Mrs. Howard.

Complaint—noisy music outside room—Mrs. Howard.

Please screen calls. Being annoyed by someone—Mrs. Howard.

"*Gotham!*" said Beth. "That clinches it!"

"What's CB CH?" said Link.

She consulted the sheet. "Complimentary fruit basket and champagne—and it comes just before the complaint about *Gotham*! Wish this thing gave the days—I'm assuming the complaints are listed in the order they came in."

"What's this about screening calls?" said Link.

"Zip?"

"I doubt it. It's so far down it must have come in after Zip was murdered."

"And the complaint about service," said Beth. "That must have been after they got the blackmail note, when they were all in a frenzy."

"What does it tell us that's new?" said Link.

"Screening calls, for one thing—wish we could find out about that. And Carlotta's a big spender."

"That's new?"

Beth didn't answer. She was looking at the screen, making notes.

"Here's what I'm getting," said Link. "A different Carlotta, sensual, wanton. She likes her food warm and her room quiet—because she makes her own music. I can see her, wrapping herself in the bedspread—the old colors become her. She's tangoing to 'Night and Day.' Bruce lies in bed watching her. She sashays to the closet, hangs up her new dresses. She does a fandango to the phone, calls the beauty—"

"You're crazy," said Beth.

"Could you learn to love a writer?"

"Could you bring up Suzy and Burt?"

The computer showed that the Brenemans had been coming to the Royal for eleven years. Like the Howards, they preferred to be up high, with an ocean view, but they took a room, not a suite. The comments list was shorter.

Provide extra hangers.
Provide cart for clothes.
$$$$$—beauty salon—Mrs. Breneman.
$$$$$—gift shop—Mrs. Breneman.
$$$$$$—dress shop—Mrs. Breneman.
Celebrity complaint—Mrs. Breneman annoying.
CB CH
Complaint—magazine to be forwarded has not arrived—Mr. Breneman.
Request wedge pillow for Mrs. Breneman.
Request bed board for Mr. Breneman.
Request more pillows—Mrs. Breneman.
Request extra blankets—Mrs. Breneman.
Complaint. Overcharge on breakfast—Mr. Breneman.
Request ironing board—Mrs. Breneman.

"Look," Beth said excitedly. "Right after the fruit and champagne. Burt wanted to see *Gotham.*"

"You don't know it's *Gotham.* Hey, Suzy's a big spender too. Even more than Carlotta. And look at those requests—keeps the maid busy."

Beth was jotting down notes. "The complaint about the bill," she said. "That's just like Burt."

"I suspect Burt is something of a twentieth-century Helmer," said Link.

"Is Suzy a Nora?"

"In a way. I can imagine her begging like a squirrel when she wants money. Or maybe she does extra ironing for him. Suzy ironing—hard to believe."

"Nora wanted to leave the doll's house," said Beth. "She wanted to go out there somewhere—anywhere. Does Suzy strike you that way?"

"Here's how Suzy strikes me—how they both strike me. They sleep badly. They're desperate—they try new pillows, more blankets, a bed board. Nothing helps. I see them tossing in bed. Can't sleep, says Burt. It's your bed board, says Suzy. I'll get up and iron it—but that means an extra stop in the dress shop. Now, Suzy, he says, ironing's your job anyway. That's like . . . like blackmailing your own husband. It would be different, she says, if you were a celebrity. But I am a celebrity, he says. What about the loophole? No, she says. It's not the same. She stares outside, thinking about real celebrities: a rock star, a football player, a—"

"A famous writer," said Beth. "You've got a miniseries going."

"Could you learn to love someone who writes for television?"

"I might—if he gets back to the computer. Could you bring up Twinky and Doc?"

Twinky and Doc had been coming to the Royal for twelve years. As long as it was high up with an ocean view, the room they stayed in didn't seem to matter. The comment list was short.

QR
CP
Mrs. Delorio is allergic to peanut oil.
CB CH
Guest complaint—Mr. Delorio noisy at dinner.
Request change to twin beds—Mrs. Delorio.
Complaint—Food in Islands Room made her ill—Mrs. Delorio.

They consulted the sheet and discovered that QR meant request quiet room and CP meant cheese platter in the room.

"The complaint about Twinky being noisy," said Link. "That came after the champagne. The tension period," he said in a mock-dramatic tone.

"And the request for twin beds," she said, jotting it down. "That came after the champagne too."

"Trouble sleeping?" said Link.

"Trouble getting along?" said Beth. "Maybe they had a fight. I wonder. . . . Is it possible Doc didn't know about Twinky?"

"And I wonder what's cooked in peanut oil. What do you suppose Doc had for dinner that night? What did we have? Beth? Beth? This is Link. Do you read me?"

She came out of her trance. "Sorry . . . I was thinking about something. Link, can you bring up Bruce and Carlotta again?"

She stared at the screen for some time. "What's so interesting?" Link asked.

"I'm trying to remember . . ."

"Remember what?" The phone rang.

"Don't answer!"

But Link had picked up automatically.

"What the hell's taking so long?" said Sig.

"We're just leaving."

"Have you found out anything?"

"Get off the phone!" said Beth.

"Maybe. We'll be right up."

The second time in an hour. The operator debated. . . . No, she decided, it's too late for the cleaning crew. She flashed Security. "Something's going on in the concierge's office."

Softly they closed the door behind them.

Link looked at her. "You remembered!"

She nodded. "I know more about who. I still have some questions. But—"

"But you're sure about who!" He stopped in front of a Japanese screen. "Tell me!"

"Later. Let's get out of here."

"Right," said Link. "Sig's going nuts. We'd better get up before—"

"Just a minute," came a voice from the far side of the lobby. One of the guards they had seen earlier.

"You go ahead, Beth," said Link. "I'll take care of this."

"But why should you . . . ?"

She hesitated. She did not want to explain herself to the guard now. She wasn't sure she had enough to tell the police.

"Go!" Link gave her a push. Then he turned and went to meet the guard. "What's up?" he said casually.

Beth made for the stairs. Behind her she heard the guard say, "Where are the others?"

"What others? Listen, I have a complaint. I thought the concierge was on duty around the clock. In a hotel like this, when the guests are trapped inside, you ought to make the Nautilus machines available twenty-four hours a day! No concierge to ask! No one at the desk!" Link ranted on with threats to call Bucky. The guard stared at him as if he were a lunatic.

Someone moved away from the screen and walked rapidly in the direction Beth had taken.

CHAPTER
37

Beth paused on the stairs and saw Link and the guard crossing the lobby. Link was talking and waving his arms, pantomiming something. Beth smiled to herself, wondering what fantasy he was spinning for the guard. She watched until they had moved out of sight, then continued upward, thinking about her discovery. She stopped, took out her notebook, and read over some jottings. Yes, she was certain. But why would—? Footsteps sounded behind her.

She looked over her shoulder. My God! Was it possible? Waiting for me? "Oh, hi. You're up late too," she said, with a jollity that sounded fake even to her.

Couldn't sleep, was the reply. They continued up the stairs together, talking about the weather, speculating about when it would break, all the while Beth thinking—had she made a mistake? Should she have gone back to Link and the guard?

Too late now. She glanced around. Usually, even at this hour, a few night owls would be returning from the terrace bar or a walk on the beach. But weather—and terror—had kept everyone in, and she saw a panorama of emptiness. To her left and right were silent corridors, the only human sight, pairs of shoes left out to be cleaned. Far ahead through the atrium, where rain fell steadily on the trees, she could see the East stairway. No one.

But maybe she was wrong to feel uneasy. She turned to her companion. Their eyes met. In one deadly instant, friendship shattered—and Beth knew. Her companion was lying in wait.

Quickly Beth moved up a few steps. She broke into a run. A moment's pause, then she heard feet pounding behind her. The playacting was over.

Should she go up to Sig? Too many flights. She'd never make it. She reached a landing—hesitated a second—then left the stairs, rushing past the shuttered doors. Behind her, footsteps sounded on the tile. Should she knock on a door? What if they refused to open? She ran headlong down the corridor, banged into a railing. She looked down at the drop to the courtyard and forced herself ahead. She reached the elevators. Was there time? No! Her best chance was to get back to the lobby. She dashed past another set of doors to the East stairway.

Down she plunged, flight after flight. Once she looked back— gaining on her! She ran on, reached bottom, turned toward the lobby—and froze, disoriented. Ahead of her was the promenade courtyard. Oh God! She had gone down one flight too many.

She sprinted past dark shops, walls of art, shields, war masks— bizarre. Not as bizarre as the mask her pursuer had been assuming. Faster. Go faster. In the wall—she had almost missed it—a door. She opened it and sped through.

She found herself in a winding corridor, hospitallike, white walls, white tile. She plunged ahead, reached another corridor— and halted. Which way to go?

Behind her, a door slammed against the wall. Hoping her pursuer would go the other way, she sprinted to the right. She dashed past tall metal cages with racks of glasses, blue and white dishes. She must be back of the house: the main vein of the hotel. She rushed ahead. There had to be another exit to the outside.

She tore down the corridor, stopping at a glass door. She slid it open, saw a U-shaped counter holding computers, menus, telephones. Room Service. If only they stayed open all night.

Feet pounding on the tile, coming up fast.

She rushed to a phone, yanked the receiver off and left it dangling. Then she ran through the room and through another door, slamming it shut. She stumbled around a clump of service carts, heard the pounding feet almost upon her.

She shot past tall carved chests that held chafing dishes, familiar tablecloths. She must be back of the Raffia. A deafening bang. She turned, saw her pursuer burst out of Room Service. She looked ahead, saw tanks of lobsters, abalone, sea urchins like round brushes, clinging to the glass walls. Gasping for breath, she ran to a tank and stood behind it, facing her pursuer.

"Here! Down here!" she called. Her voice bounced off the walls and echoed down the corridor.

"Silly. They'll never hear you," said Suzy.

She was not even winded. The floppy doll had transmuted into an amazon. An amazon in a romper outfit, bloodred, red as the rolled-up *Gotham* she carried under one arm. Her arms, her legs—why had Beth never noticed? Not chubby—brawny, muscles gleaming under the bright light. She stared, saw Suzy tighten her grip on the magazine, saw something glinting inside.

"You found out," said Suzy. "How?" The same little-girl voice, but the Raggedy Ann features were contorted into a look of such hatred that Beth felt a chill of terror.

"*The Prince and the Pauper.* That got me started," Beth said, her hands inching up, searching for the rim of the tank.

"A professor. I knew I'd made a mistake the minute I said it."

"Your friend Keke?" said Beth, knowing the answer, playing for time. The phone was off the hook. The operator had to notice.

"Yes—Keke! She loved helping me play my little prank. I dressed her up in my outfit: 'Something bright, Keke, something my friends will see and know it's mine. Now go down for coffee —and if you do it right, everyone will think you're me. Twins! Isn't this fun?' "

"And then you . . . ?"

"I took a shortcut over the golf course."

Stall. The phone's off the hook. "But Zip was so much bigger. How could you . . . ?"

"Easy as pie. I told him I'd lost a contact." Suzy giggled. "I wanted to laugh in his face. He looked so serious, on his hands and knees, pulling the grass apart—all bent over. Perfect!" she said with girlish enthusiasm. She might have been talking about her lucky find of exactly the right chintz for the sofa. "Same thing with Twinky. 'Good old Suzy—I'll find your contact.' Perfect!" she repeated. She lifted an arm—paused—then slammed it down with brute force.

Heart beating wildly, Beth held tight to the glass tank. "That night in the Islands Room. Bruce and Carlotta, Twinky and Doc— they were dancing. You sent Burt up for your sweater. Then you were alone at the table. You had time."

"Time to monkey a little with Doc's dinner," said Suzy. "Clever, Professor." She fingered the magazine.

The phone is off the hook. Can't be much longer. "How did you know about me?"

"That day in the beauty shop. I could tell you didn't think Eleanor Lunette's death was an accident. I knew you had your suspicions too. And I knew your type—one of those achieving women who never lets go. The type that pokes her nose into things that are none of her business. After . . . after Zip, I kept an eye on you. I saw you looking inside Zip's office. I saw you looking at the *Gotham*s. Did you think I'd let some . . . some *professor* stop me?" The loathing in her voice was like a stab. "I've been planning this for a year."

"Then you knew about Zip before . . . ?" The operator *must* have noticed.

"Before this year? Of course. I always know when Burt's hiding something. He's so . . . so . . . transparent. Good word, Professor? I made him tell me everything. Then I pretended I didn't understand. 'But Burt, dear' "—high, puzzled voice—" 'why are you worrying? Even if this silly person who's bothering you did tell her, why would she mind? You did all the work. She wouldn't have time to write anyway, not on maternity leave.' I pretended to forget all about it. Gave a party for a big client. The caterers left a knife behind, sharper than anything I had, sharp as a razor. I kept it—but for who? Who was the bastard trying to wreck my life? Then last year I was taking a lesson, and Zip let something slip about Apple Tree, New Jersey. He caught himself—didn't think I noticed. Poor, dumb Suzy. He probably thought I didn't even know about Burt, and we left a few days later." A hand reached inside the magazine.

"But why . . . ?" Where the hell was Security?

"Why did I wait? I had to get ready. The minute we got home from the Royal I started my . . . my regimen. Right word, Professor? Joined a club and got my own personal trainer. Told him I wanted to protect myself against rapists. He worked me like hell. Just what I wanted. Every time Burt sent money to that bastard I knew it, and I worked harder. Burt didn't notice." She giggled. "No one noticed. Same old lazybones Suzy. Life can be so simple when everyone thinks you're a dumb bunny." Another giggle—

steeped in poison. "Even a dumb bunny *knows to put the phone back.*" She pulled out the knife, let the magazine drop.

Beth gripped the tank. *Wait.* She watched Suzy move toward her. *Not yet.* Suzy started a dash around the tank. Summoning all her power, Beth shoved. The tank teetered uncertainly, then toppled, clipping Suzy's shoulder as it crashed to the floor, releasing a Niagara of water and lobsters. Suzy cried out, fell into the water. A fleeting image of Suzy, staggering up, slipping back, large red claws crawling over her thighs.

Water cascaded over the corridor, slapping the walls. Beth sloshed through, skidded. Below her, an arm thrust out. A hand grasped her ankle. She kicked Suzy's arm. Suzy screamed and let go. Beth leaped past and went slipping and sliding down the corridor. She reached a dry spot and broke into a run. She sped by storage rooms, employee rest rooms—if only someone would come out. She shot around a corner. From behind a door—voices! She was safe. She tried the door. It opened!

Her heart sank. She was in the video room. On the screen a black-and-white movie was playing grotesquely to rows of empty chairs.

A train whistle.

"I know there's a Miss Froy. She's as real as you are."

"That's what you say and you believe it, but there doesn't appear to be anyone else who's seen her."

The Lady Vanishes—she could recite it backward and forward. Outside she heard running. It suddenly hit her that she was going to die, here in this empty room with her favorite movie playing in the background. She thought with regret of things half-finished or never started, the books she had meant to write, the love she had meant to have. She went to the far side of the room and stood

under the screen. The door crashed open. Beyond the sea of unoc-
cupied chairs, Suzy looked at her triumphantly.

*"They're lying. But why? Why? Listen, Miss Froy was on that train.
I know she was."*

Suzy came toward her, knocking chairs aside. Beth stared at the
knife that glinted in her hand.

"You could have come forward," Beth said desperately. "You
could have told everyone Zip was a blackmailer."

Suzy's soft features seemed to dissolve, then harden into lines
of rage. "And let everyone know about Burt?" she exploded. "Do
you really think I want to change lives with Keke—that I want to
be the pauper and not the prince!" She stumbled on, pushing
through the chairs.

Train wheels squealing.
"Would you like a little air?"
"Yes."
"Think you can eat anything?"
"I could try."

The dialogue, so familiar. In a minute the screen would show—
an idea flashed across her mind. Could she do it? Could she hold
Suzy off until the right moment? Suzy lurched toward her.
Quickly Beth surveyed the room, working out a path through the
chairs. Then, eyes on Suzy, she said with all the sarcasm she
could muster, "What did *you* do to deserve your life, Suzy Breneman?"

Suzy stopped as if she'd been struck. "What did I do? I did
everything!"

"Harriman's Herbal Tea! She said it was the only sort she liked."

Almost there. "Like what?" said Beth. "Burt's the lawyer—he did everything."

"Burt?" Suzy screamed. "Did Burt go to house sales so we could furnish on a shoestring? Did Burt buy the birthday presents for his mother? Did Burt give the parties for the clients? Where was Burt when the roof leaked? Where was Burt when the Principal called us in? He was where he always was—at his office—and he almost ruined everything. And you—you want to ruin everything too!" She kicked a chair out of the way and charged ahead.

"My father was a very remarkable man."
"Did he play the clarinet?"

Hurry, hurry, Beth thought, listening desperately to the dialogue.

"You know why you fascinate me? I'll tell you. You have two great qualities I used to admire in Father. You haven't any manners at all and you're always seeing things. Well, what's the matter?"

Get ready. On the screen, the train passed through a tunnel. Suddenly the video room turned pitch black *Now!* Beth lunged for the path.

"Miss Froy's name on the window. You must have seen it! Stop the train!"

Wedged in the middle, Suzy turned heavily, changed direction. Pitching chairs aside, she staggered toward Beth. Racing for her life, Beth ran for the door.

"Please help me! Please make them stop the train!"

Beth tore out of the room.

She ran ahead and through an open doorway. She was in the kitchen. Glorious, she had heard it called. Don't make them this big anymore. Don't make them with a place to hide. Vast counters, all clear. On the far side of the room, a huge dishwasher, the size of a small hallway. She ran to it. Could she crawl inside? Pounding feet—Suzy rushed into the kitchen.

Beth crouched behind the dishwasher, watched Suzy look around the dark room, watched her circle the counters. She spotted Beth and ran toward her.

Beth jumped up, raced out of the kitchen and turned a sharp right. She was in a narrow passage with rows of heavy wooden doors. She opened one, felt a blast of cold air, saw shelves stocked with meat. She opened another—eggs and milk. She opened another door, left it slightly ajar, heard running, and heaved at the door. With a loud click it jammed shut. Immediately she felt a wave of terror. This was what it was like to be buried alive. Tomorrow they would open the door and find her frozen corpse.

She looked around, almost screamed. Staring down from the shelves were fantastic figures, carved in ice: a scorpion, a lion, a crab. A glacial zodiac. They were all here. Taurus. Aries. Sagittarius, the archer, prepared to shoot his arrow. She would become one of the ice figures, a frozen thing. Or else she would die by Suzy's hand. She heard a door open and bang shut. In a few moments Suzy would pull this door open. No escape.

Then she saw the sign. THIS REFRIGERATOR DOOR IS EQUIPPED WITH AN INSIDE SAFETY RELEASE. YOU CANNOT BE LOCKED IN. She hoped it was true. But did she dare go out?

She waited, shivering in her T-shirt and shorts. She had been sweaty, but now her flesh was covered with goose bumps, her body shaking. She took a deep breath, inhaled icy air, and listened. Not a sound. She's waiting, hoping I'll stay inside and die. But if I go out, she'll be ready.

Minutes went by. Her body was a block of ice. She felt herself getting sleepy. No! She would rather go out and face Suzy than die alone in this icy tomb.

She pulled the handle and felt a surge of panic. The door would not move. Frantically, she wrenched the handle up and down. The door started to give. She kicked the bottom. The door opened with a loud creak. She held it open a few inches, peered out—nothing. Oh, the air—so warm. *Don't go out yet. Get a weapon.* She went back, stood on a storage tub, and reached for Sagittarius. Her hand slithered up, then froze to the arrow. She ripped her hand away. With numb and bleeding fingers, she tore off her T-shirt. She wrapped it around the archer, leaving bow and arrow exposed.

One arm holding the archer—God, it weighed a ton!—the other on the door, slowly, slowly, she pushed. Then she opened the door all the way. Suzy!

She lunged for Beth, knife aimed at her chest.

Beth held the archer in front of her, using it as a shield. Ice sprayed through the air as she knocked the knife out of Suzy's hand. The knife careened against the wall. Suzy yelled and went after it. Beth blocked her. Pointing the arrow ahead, she hit Suzy in the stomach. With a sharp crack the arrow broke off, and bits of ice cut into Beth's face, as Suzy gasped and doubled over. With all her strength Beth slammed the mangled archer down on Suzy. She dropped to the floor and lay still.

Down the hall, Beth saw figures running toward her. Was it Sig and Link? She tried to say, "What took you so long?" The figures blurred. Her head was a spinning merry-go-round, lights going on and off. She sank into darkness.

CHAPTER
38

"Suzy, you didn't have to . . . do that." Burt's voice, almost pleading.

"Do what?" Suzy's voice, as cold as the inside of a refrigerator.

Beth opened her eyes, looked up at the ceiling. The light from the fluorescents was blinding. She closed her eyes. She ached all over, as if she had been battered. This must be what it was like to wake up on the operating table when the anesthetic had worn off too soon.

"You know—Zip." Burt again. "That wasn't like you—to do a thing like that. I didn't even know you knew. How did you know?"

"The note," said Suzy.

"What note?"

"Zip sent you a note with the champagne. I got to it before you."

Beth lay there listening, aware of waves of air over her face, of something soft on her arm. She wanted to say something but couldn't seem to get the words out.

"The bastard." Suzy laughed. "I'm glad I did it."

"You mean . . . what you . . . did to Zip?"

"Twinky. I'm glad I put his Rolex in the Buddha. Thought he was so smart, always rubbing the Buddha's belly for luck. Well, he ran out of luck."

"But *why*, Suzy—why Twinky?"

No answer. Beth opened her eyes again, saw Sig standing above her, fanning her with a magazine. With great effort she turned her head. Link was crouched next to her, his hand on her wrist. They were staring at Suzy, who sat, legs outstretched, back to the wall. Burt stood at her side, looking miserable and strangely vulnerable, stripped of authority. It's the pajamas, Beth thought. The top was unbuttoned, exposing a chest of gray hair. His bare legs were like two sticks. "Suzy," he was saying, "dearest Suzy, please tell me."

Suzy turned away, her mouth compressed. A trickle of blood ran down her face. Her eyes were on the open refrigerator. The ice figures, Beth thought vaguely. They'll melt. Someone should close the door.

"Tell me, Suzy—why Twinky?"

"Because," Beth said, surprised at how weak her voice sounded, "because she thought that you told Doc."

Sig jumped. "Are you all right?"

Link smiled at her. "Hello," he said. "Just rest."

"That I told Doc what?" said Burt.

"That you were being blackmailed," said Beth.

"Bitch!" Suzy yelled. "How did you know he told Doc?"

"Suzy!" said Burt. "That's no way for a lady to talk."

"Something you said in the beauty shop," Beth said. She sighed. "A long time ago."

Suzy gave her a savage look and glanced at the open refrigerator. Beth knew exactly what she was thinking. If they were alone, she would grab an ice sculpture and beat her senseless.

Bucky came in, looking rumpled, shirt hanging out, bare feet in sandals. "The police are on the way," he said, and disappeared.

Suzy had turned back to Burt. "You did tell Doc, didn't you?"

"Well, all right, I did. She said she couldn't treat me until I said what was bothering me. But Suzy, Suzy." Burt knelt and took her hand. "Doc would never tell anyone."

"Fool!" She shook his hand away. "Twinky could worm anything out of Doc. And you—you're the smart one—you couldn't see what he was doing."

Burt stared. "What are you talking about?"

"Twinky's little prank. The fake interview."

"That didn't mean anything—it was a joke."

"A joke! He was ready to tell the whole world about your so-called Breneman Loophole."

"Suzy, Suzy—you did it for me." He leaned over, tried to kiss her.

"Stop kidding yourself. I did it for me," she said, moving away from him to the edge of a puddle.

There were puddles of melting ice all over the tile. Beth spotted her sodden T-shirt and suddenly remembered how she was dressed.

"Good—you're up." Bucky again—as if on cue. His shirt was tucked in, his hair neatly combed. "Thought you might want this," he said, handing a *yukata* to Beth and disappearing again.

Link helped her into the robe, a faint look of amusement on his face.

"Put it in a book," she said.

He laughed. "Never—too precious to share."

"When you leave, could you go around the back." Bucky's voice in the corridor. "And try to keep it quiet."

Then heavy footsteps, coming toward them.

"We can fight this, Suzy," said Burt. "We have a case. You're not well. You didn't know what you were doing. You don't even understand about taxes. It's like . . . like . . ."

"Oh, shut up," Suzy said.

CHAPTER
39

SUNDAY

In the Raffia kitchen, the pastry chef was beating egg whites for a chocolate soufflé that would be *à point*—perfection. At the golf course, the maids were adorning the ladies' locker room with gardenias and orchids. The storm had ended and the jubilant staff was desperate to pamper the guests.

The guests, liberated from their posh prison, had been up and out since sunrise. At the beach the surfers surfed, and the sunners, making up for lost time, heroically offered their bodies to the ultraviolet rays.

At the tennis pavilion, the courts were filled. All the pros, including Zip's replacement, were giving lessons. A round-robin was in progress and Beth sat watching the play from the terrace.

Yesterday's depression had lifted, and she felt restless, impatient to get on the courts. But she had been ordered to take it easy.

"Lilikoi juice," said Link, setting a glass in front of her. "Better known as Hawaiian truth serum. Drink up—and you'll tell all."

She took a sip. "It's working! I can feel it! What do you want to know?"

"How do you like my book?"

She flushed. "Haven't started it yet."

"A jest. Your time has been occupied with quashing criminals. What I really want to know is how you figured out it was Suzy."

"Oh that. It began when I thought back to the beauty shop and remembered Suzy questioning Doc. Suzy was so . . . urgent. It seemed so important to her to know if Doc told Twinky about her patients. When I thought about Doc's emphasis on personal problems, and remembered that she had examined Burt . . . Well, I was sure Suzy thought that he had confided in Doc, and that she also thought—"

"That Doc had told Twinky?" Beth nodded. "Very good, Professor, but how did you know about Suzy and Keke?"

"The managers' party."

Link protested that Beth had said she hadn't learned anything at the party.

"Not till I went over it in my mind. Then I remembered Suzy said she'd been reading *The Prince and the Pauper*."

"You're such a literary detective," said Link, giving her a look of admiration.

"Anyway," said Beth, her eyes on the tennis match, "that reminded me how I was struck by the resemblance between Suzy and her friend Keke. Put it together with Prince Edward and Tom Canty—"

" 'Doff thy rags and don these splendors, lad!' "

"You're pretty literary yourself, Lowenstein."

"See what you think when you've read my book."

His book again. She was almost afraid to read it.

"Okay," Link was saying. "You have Suzy doing two dress-up acts on Keke—one for Zip, one for Twinky—so she has time to get down to the trail. But how could she be sure Twinky would be alone?"

"That's why the computer records were so useful."

"Why is that, Professor Hawkshaw? I saw them too."

"Doc's allergy—remember? Suzy must have known about it. And remember the night before Twinky's murder? The whole group was at dinner. . . ." And Beth explained.

"Are you saying," Link asked, "that Suzy brought a vial of peanut oil to put in Doc's dinner?"

"Maybe. Or she might have ordered something cooked in peanut oil and then put something from her plate in Doc's food."

"What if Twinky had decided to stay in with Doc?"

"God, how I wish he had!"

"Some reunion," said Link. "Think I'll cancel my plans."

"For what?"

"My college reunion—can't remember which year."

"Try some truth serum," said Beth. Then she said, "I wonder what's going to happen to Burt. I saw him sitting on the beach this morning, just staring at the ocean."

The first set completed, the round-robin couples were crowding around the tennis desk. "Scores everyone?" said Gail. There was a chorus of "Do we have to say them out loud?" "If you'd only guarded the alley . . ." "If you'd just run up to the net with me . . ."

"Mixed doubles means mixed troubles," said a deep voice.

"Here's Sig," said Link. "He'll be able to tell you about Burt."

"Anything, sweetheart." He gave Beth a hug. "What do you want to know?"

Beth asked if the police would take Burt into custody too.

"No," said Sig, "but he'll have to stay. He's a material witness.

Even if Suzy exculpates him, they'll call him in as an accomplice. The police won't believe Suzy was protecting Burt's interests all by herself."

"That's the point," said Beth. "Suzy was protecting her interests. You know, Sig, she knew all about Burt. She told me he stole the loophole idea from someone on maternity leave."

"Ironic," said Sig, "considering Burt was so anti half-time women. I'm surprised he'd credit any of them with having an idea worth stealing."

"Credit is right. Will the police do anything about that?"

"The woman would have to file a civil suit—and she'd need proof. It gets complicated with questions of how much was original and how much was stolen. So Burt may luck out with his loophole."

"It still doesn't seem possible," said Link, "that Suzy had the strength to do all that running, and then to—"

"Strength! I was such an idiot!" said Sig.

"What do you mean?" said Beth.

"I remember seeing Suzy swimming laps like she was trying out for the Olympics, but it went right by me at the time."

"Another thing," said Link. "We still don't know how Zip notified his victims about the *Gotham* code. And we only have guesses about how he learned their secrets."

"The code wouldn't have been hard," said Beth. "One anonymous phone call to tell them where to look and what the numbers mean. . . . Hi, Gail."

Gail joined them and introduced the new pro. Blond, young, exuberant, he was ecstatic about his job—mind-boggling to be at the Royal, awesome facilities. They talked for a while and then the pro asked Gail if he could get a new phone directory. "Look at this one," he said, "notes and stuff all over it."

"What kind of notes?" said Beth.

"I'm not sure—they're not tennis scores. Just numbers and letters."

"Can I have a look?"

"Sure—keep it." He went off to set up a lesson, and Gail returned to the round-robin.

Sig and Link looked over her shoulder while Beth examined the directory.

"Come clean, Beth," said Sig. "You have an idea about those numbers."

"Just a guess, but they look like the three-digit codes for picking up answering machine messages. That's one way Zip could get the dirt on his friends. All he had to do was watch them make a call, see what numbers they pushed to get messages, and note them down. From then on, whenever he wanted—"

"He could pick up urgent messages," said Link, "recorded sales talks, dentist appointments."

"What if there were calls like 'When are you going to give me credit for my idea?' Or 'When are you going to share the money that belongs to me?' "

"Or," said Link, " 'When are you going to make this year's contribution to PBS?' "

"Doubter," said Beth. "I'm going to find out." She went to the tennis desk, looked at the number marked *H,* and picked up the phone. Two rings, a few bars of "It Was Just One of Those Things," then Carlotta's voice. "The Howards are out dancing now, but please, please, leave a message. We're dying to talk to you." A beep. At once Beth pushed the three-digit number. A series of beeps. "Mrs. Howard, I'm so excited. Your Chanel is in. Please call Sophie." Beep. "Here is Esperanza again, Mr. Howard. You say you help me and the childrens after Carlos die. You enjoy his money and all I ask is what Carlos deserve. I am citizen now and I got lawyer. The lawyer say we prove . . . periodic verbal agreement. So you let me know right away what you do, or my lawyer, he take steps."

"That clinches it!" Beth called out triumphantly, looked up— and quickly replaced the receiver.

"Clinches what?" said Carlotta as she swept out of the pro shop, followed by Bruce. She had a way of making an entrance as if she expected an ovation. She almost deserved one for her flowing leopard-print pajamas, and Bruce, too, for his safari outfit out of Banana Republic. "Clinches what?" Carlotta repeated, staring at the phone.

"Just calling for the weather," said Link.

"Checking my plane reservation," said Beth.

Carlotta looked suspiciously from Beth to Link. "My! Shouldn't you get your stories straight?" Link mumbled something about two phone calls. He sounded so unconvincing that Bruce gave him a sharp look and seemed ready to join the interrogation.

Sig saved the day with "That's a pretty lei, Carlotta."

"Like it? They made me a special one for going away." Then, sensing an unfortunate ambiguity—"I mean a going-away lei."

Were the Howards leaving? they asked.

"On the road again," said Bruce. "Stopping at home first—have some business to take care of. Then we're off to Hong Kong."

"No, we're not," said Carlotta. "The shopping in Rome is much better. We came to see if Doc was here—wanted to say good-bye. Where is Doc?"

But no one had seen her.

"Oh well. We don't have much time." Fixing her eyes on Beth, Carlotta said, "Did you enjoy your talk with the police?"

Her voice was so frosty that Beth was sure Carlotta knew she had told the police her suspicions. "I thought the police were . . . reasonable," said Beth.

"Reasonable! They were insolent! Where is that limo, Bruce?"

And there it was, a white stretch, perilously navigating the

walk between the courts. It pulled to a stop at the bougainvillea
hedge, and a uniformed driver emerged. He took the Howards'
hand luggage—Vuitton, real, not faux—and placed it inside the
limousine.

They said good-bye, Carlotta graciously tendering a cheek to
the men. "Come on, Bruce." She started for the limo. "Oh, wait."
She removed her lei. "Ruins the look," she said, tossing the lei
into a basket of used towels. "Well, aloha and all that."

Failing an attempt to make a three-point turn, but succeeding in
crushing the hedge, the limousine backed off. A window rolled
down and Carlotta's head appeared. "God, would you believe it
about Suzy?" she called. "And she played such lousy tennis."

"And so it ends," said Link. "The reunion from hell."

"But heaven to see them depart," said Sig.

"What about Bruce and Carlotta?" Beth asked Sig. "The police
told me they said they didn't know anything about blackmail.
And when I told the police about the lottery, they weren't interested."

"They wouldn't be—it's out of their hands. That's a civil case
too. And the other person would have to sue."

"That would be Esperanza," said Beth. "I suspect she's the
business Bruce has to take care of at home." She told them about
the message. "I'm betting that Carlos was the systems person and
when he died Bruce decided to keep all the winnings. But Esperanza sounds tough. Carlotta and Bruce may have to delay their
travels. I certainly hope so."

"Carlotta kissed Suzy off in a hurry," said Link.

"Just the same," said Beth, "I feel sorry for Suzy."

For God's sake, they said, why?

"Of all three women, Suzy was the one to whom what her
husband did mattered the most. Carlotta has her money, or thinks
she has, and Doc has her practice. But Suzy—and he helped her
believe it—saw herself as nothing without Burt. It wasn't just his

income—it was the prestige. Everything that mattered to her—prominence, social standing, reputation—depended on Burt. She's like a wife in a nineteenth-century novel, a *Middlemarch* wife."

"Like Mrs. Bulstrode?" said Link.

"More like Rosamond Lydgate—obsessed with social position."

"But Burt is nothing like Lydgate."

"Hardly," said Beth. "Lydgate—poor devil—was a true thinker. Burt is Casaubon, forever accumulating knowledge—and incapable of forming an original idea."

"If you're going to talk about *Middlemarch,*" said Sig, "I'll see you later. I have to pack."

"Pack?" said Beth. "You have two whole days."

"Changed my mind. I'm leaving tomorrow night. I have some new plans," he said, a look of suppressed excitement on his face.

What plans? they asked. What was so pressing?

"I'm going home." He paused. Then with surprising energy he said, "I'm going to file a suit against my firm."

Delighted, they gave him a round of applause. Then Beth said, "What actually happened, Sig? You said something about being kicked upstairs."

"What happened is that they made me 'of counsel,' which means I was put on a stipend—and left without work. They said it was a constructive discharge to make room for a younger person. What it means is I got too expensive for them. They could hire someone younger for peanuts."

"That younger person argument," said Beth. "It's so irrational. Give them time and they have the same chance you had."

"They said I wasn't bringing in as many clients," Sig said angrily. "Of course I wasn't bringing in profit—but that was because they weren't using me. I was just hitting my stride as a rainmaker."

"There was a professor I knew," said Beth. "A magnificent

teacher. And Midwestern forced retirement on him when he still had so much to offer."

"What grounds will you use, Sig?" said Link.

"Age discrimination. I've got some great precedents. And there's a lawsuit pending in Chicago that could help enormously. It's a tough case to win—but I'm going to do it." He took his feet off the table and sat up straight. "Either they bring me back to where I was, or there will be no firm. I helped found it—I'll un-found it!" A sigh. "But I'd rather go back to work."

"That professor," said Beth. "He came to the library for a while, said he was writing a book. Then I saw him less and less."

"Gave up and faded away," said Link. "I've seen it too."

"Do it, Sig," said Beth. "Work! 'How dull it is to pause, to make an end, To rust unburnish'd, not to shine in use! As tho' to breathe were life!' "

"Osumi?" said Sig.

"Tennyson," said Link, "and he's with you all the way. 'To strive, to seek, to find, and not to yield.' "

"Not to yield, eh? My sentiments exactly," said Sig. "And good, even if it's not Osumi."

"Give em hell, Sig," said Link, and the three stood and exchanged high fives to the amusement of the kids playing on the near court. Beth thought back to their first exchange and of how much had happened in between.

"See you at dinner," said Sig. They watched him move up the winding path, walking confidently, almost swaggering. He reached the steps and went up rapidly, running the last few.

A short time later Link and Beth went up the same path. They paused as they entered the lobby. A circle of guests, wearing leis, stood listening to a guide. "The philosophy of the Royal," the guide was saying, "is do whatever it takes to make a guest happy. There is no bottom line. Notice the front desk. It's simple, under-stated, to give the feeling the hotel is a home. The same is true for the individual lights above the door of each room. Whenever you're here, you're at home. Guests come to think of this place as home. Here at the Royal, we have a very high percentage of returns. . . ."

"Will you come back?" Link asked Beth.

"Definitely."

"You haven't changed your mind about when you're leaving?"

"No. I'm staying on until Wednesday."

"Good. So am I. After Sig leaves—not that I'm rushing him—we'll have one whole day together."

"All of Tuesday," said Beth. "I love Tuesdays."

As they entered the elevator, someone asked the guide, "Is there a place to jog?"

The doors closed and they never heard the answer.

CHAPTER
40

In days to come, when Beth thought back to that Tuesday, she always started with their morning walk. Without discussion, they had kept away from the jogging trail and roamed the grounds.

She remembered discovering an unexpected garden, dense with fantastic flowers, like a romantic jungle. She remembered sitting on the bench at the famous ninth hole, watching the golfers try for the green and hit balls into the sea. She remembered their stop at the luau courtyard, where they had stumbled on Bucky, giving a pep talk to row upon row of employees. He was reminding them of the Royal's triumphs—food and service had won the Golden Salver, the golf course the Golden Tee, the tennis facilities the Golden Racket. "And our Golden Lei," he said. "We're the number one resort, not just in the state, but in the world." Someone asked a question. They couldn't hear the words, but they heard Bucky's reply. "Yes," he said, "We *will* re-bless."

She remembered strolling the beach, counting how many people were reading Link's books, until Link made her stop. She remembered sitting in lounge chairs, holding hands.

It was then that Doc had come to say good-bye. Dressed for travel, face drawn but composed, she told them her plane would leave in a few hours. "I went out running the other night," she said. "I got drenched—but I didn't care. I couldn't stop thinking about Twinky, about how much he loved the Royal, how he always hated to leave. And now . . ." She stopped, her face working to keep back the tears. "It's so pointless," she said presently. "I never told Twinky about Burt—or any of my patients. . . . And that other . . . thing," she said, looking at them closely. "I know you know about it. Please . . . don't judge Twinky. For years he was head of the agency's creative team, and he developed so many wonderful projects. Then . . . it was just one slip. I'm still proud of him." But the look of disappointment on her face refuted her words.

It must be hard, Beth thought, to accept even one lapse in honor, when Doc herself was so straightforward. "Another disillusioned wife," she said to Link after Doc left. "It's *Middlemarch* again."

"You're thinking of Mrs. Bulstrode."

"Of course, but there's also Rosamond. She marries a doctor so she can have the life she's always wanted. With Lydgate, she'll move up in society, mingle with the aristocracy, and have scads of money—she thinks. What she gets is a husband who watches every penny. And then—good-bye, aristocracy—he becomes involved in a scandal that forces them out of town."

"Yes," said Link, "but—"

"And there's Dorothea." Beth steamrolled on. "She's desperate to educate herself. So she marries Casaubon, thinking she'll be saved from ignorance by helping a brilliant man with his life's work. Instead she finds herself partnered with an egoistic, petty fool! And his work!—the work he said would be a 'great harvest of truth'—turns out to be trivial, valueless." Beth picked up a handful of sand and let it run through her fingers. "Some education!"

"Okay," said Link, "but you're forgetting the disillusioned husbands. Lydgate thinks Rosamond has just the intelligence he wants. She'll be at his side, helping him win fame through his research. What he gets is a shallow wife who doesn't care a hoot about his scientific messing around. And what about poor Casaubon? He thinks he's got himself an adoring bride. She'll worship him—and his work. Instead he's saddled with a wife whose mind is vastly superior to his. He knows she sees his flaws. Worse—he knows she's sharp enough to see the flaws in his work."

"I still feel for Dorothea the most," said Beth. "Beginning with her disappointment in Casaubon's work—"

"Let's go for a swim," said Link.

She remembered the afternoon on the terrace. Thinking ahead to Midwestern and the start of classes a few days after she returned, Beth said, "I hear the West-to-East jet lag is awful."

"I have just the prescription for jet lag," said Link. "One day preflight—no caffeine, two drinks, and at least three afternoon hours in a darkened room. Great preventive."

"It really works?"

"Guaranteed," he said, and ordered four Sunset Slings.

Although its effectiveness as a jet lag preventive remained to be seen, following the prescription to the letter proved highly satisfying.

She remembered getting ready for dinner, taking dresses out of the closet, trying them on, throwing them aside, until the bed was piled with clothes. Finally she opened a suitcase. The black—she had never worn it. Too clingy?

When Link saw her, he said, "You look . . . well, I am definitely not among the disillusioned."

She remembered dancing the hula on the Raffia terrace. She remembered dinner, not the food, but the long pauses, the gazes —then a woman asking Link to sign a book. She looked at him so adoringly that Beth felt—no, not jealous, just mildly annoyed at the interruption. She remembered their final toast. "To Sig—some work of noble note may yet be done," said Beth. They clinked glasses. "Sig," said Link. "May he drink life to the lees."

She remembered walking down to the flagstoned promontory where an eager crowd was waiting. "I guess they're not coming tonight," someone said. And suddenly, just as Beth and Link looked down into the floodlit ocean, there they were—the manta rays. Shining like emeralds, they frolicked in the water, then slid and swayed into their special hula for the Royal.

She remembered wandering out on the front lawn, looking up at the stars. A lecture was in progress, and the guests were taking turns looking through a telescope. She remembered standing apart, finding their own constellations, and Link saying, "The view from my lanai is spectacular."

Which it was. " 'And a heaven full of stars, Over my head, White and topaz, And misty red,' " Beth quoted.

"Polynesian stars," said Link.

"Are they different?"

"More sparkling," he said, as they left the lanai.

Much later Link said, "What you said before—that you feel the most for Dorothea. Aren't you forgetting that after Casaubon dies, when she marries Ladislaw, there's no disillusionment. They're both fulfilled."

"Maybe not disillusionment—but there's no fulfillment for Dorothea."

"Why? Ladislaw is hardly an intellectual disappointment."

"True. But what's in it for Dorothea?" She stopped. Why had Sig's face flashed into her mind? Work! For the first time, Beth realized that it was work—or lack of it—that haunted her thoughts. "When Dorothea goes to London with Ladislaw," she said, "all her energy is channeled into his work. When he becomes a Member of Parliament, all her satisfaction comes from helping him with his reforms. That's not fulfillment. That's . . ." She sat up. "When I think of a colleague who sees all the women in nineteenth-century novels as controlling, man-eating vampires, I want to—"

"Drink his blood?"

"How *could* a woman accomplish anything—except through a man? Dorothea had a fine mind—and she could only use it to help Ladislaw. What a waste! George Eliot knew it. She thought it a pity that Dorothea—'so substantial and rare a creature,' she called her—should have been known only as Ladislaw's wife. Who knows what Suzy might have—"

"You mean Dorothea."

"What did I say?"

"You said 'Suzy.' "

"I must have been thinking about her. All right. Who knows what Dorothea—or Suzy—might have become with encouragement and a decent education? But—do you remember what her uncle said?" Beth asked indignantly.

"Whose uncle? Suzy's?"

"Idiot." But she said it affectionately. "Dorothea's. Well, do you remember?"

"Not offhand," said Link, a finger tracing Beth's profile.

"I'll tell you. Her uncle said, 'We must not have you get too learned for a woman, you know.' What chance," said Beth, "did Dorothea have to find her own work? In her first marriage, she's a prisoner, captive to her husband's every asinine wish. In her second, she's a handmaiden—to her husband's vocation!"

"This may not be the right time to mention it," said Link, "but I understand the Royal has a wonderful honeymoon package."

Beth threw a pillow at him.

"Oh well," she said, calming down. "That's the way George Eliot wanted me to feel—she wrote social realism, not romance."

"I know someone who writes good romance," said Link.

"Who?"

"Me. Your pillow, I believe?"

CHAPTER
41

WEDNESDAY

The next day, shortly before it was time to leave, Beth ran down to the gift shop and bought every Lincoln Lowenstein in stock. She crammed the books inside a suitcase and called for her luggage to be picked up.

She paid her bill, silently sympathizing with the adjacent cashier, under siege from a man behaving like an IRS agent doing an audit. "Hey, I thought you were going to give me a break on the suite rate. . . . I don't remember playing golf on—" He stopped abruptly, looking around him. The hotel, as if it were playing Sleeping Beauty, had come to a standstill. The cashiers had stopped punching buttons, the bellhops had put down their luggage. Guests who had been dashing about the lobby, had stopped in their tracks.

All eyes were on the group of employees following a white-haired man in a black suit. Moving at a dignified pace, he crossed the lobby, stopped at the stairway, and stood facing the bay. The group—among them Bucky, Gail, and the new head tennis pro—watched him silently, waiting. He paused a few moments, his eyes scanning the ocean. Then he flung his arms open and began speaking in Hawaiian.

"What's he saying?" Beth whispered to Betty, next to her at the edge of the crowd.

She turned to Beth, her round face set in solemn lines. "That's the kahuna," she said. "He's blessing the Royal." Betty listened intently. "He's blessing the employees of the Royal and their families. . . . Now," she continued her running translation, "he's blessing the guests of the Royal. Now he's blessing the friends and employees of the Royal who can't be with us today. . . . Oh, now he's giving a blessing for world peace."

Beth watched the priest dip a ti leaf into a bowl of water and sprinkle droplets about the lobby. "That's Hawaiian water," said Betty, "with Hawaiian salt that's been blessed in church. A very special blessing." Her face was radiant. "Before we came up here, we went down and watched him bless the jogging trail. I heard him tell Bucky—Mr. Anderson—that ti leaves should be planted around the entrance to the trail so whatever evil spirits are there will be left behind. I feel it now," said Betty. "The Royal will never lose its special aloha."

The priest finished. The phones, which had been silent, began ringing, the IRS complainer resumed his harangue, and the bell-hops picked up the luggage and carried it out to the front entrance.

Link came to tell Beth that their car was waiting. As they started to leave, a girl ran up to Beth and held out a beautiful lei, woven of shiny green leaves. She put the lei around Beth's neck and kissed her on both cheeks. "Aloha 'oe, Miss Austin. *Kipa hou mai!* Come visit us again."

"*Mahalo,*" said Beth, "and how lovely. The fragrance is wonderful."

Maile vine, the girl told her, adding that a maile lei meant a special honor.

"But who ordered it?"

"Mr. Anderson." The girl glanced toward the ocean railing. There, next to an ornately carved Thai phoenix, stood Bucky. He waved to Beth. "Aloha, Professor. Safe journey." He looked as if he was about to say something else, but a couple who had been waiting impatiently planted themselves in front of him. "Unacceptable, Bucky . . . beds aren't facing the ocean . . . bedspreads the wrong color . . ." Beth's last sight was of an unperturbed Bucky, listening attentively, as if nothing in the world was more important to him than bedspread colors.

The car stopped at the gatehouse. "Party of two," said the driver. "Lowenstein and Austin." As the limousine followed the bending road, Beth looked out the window, storing up memories of tropical beauty against winter in Chicago. They passed a wall with the Royal logo carved in stone, and turned onto the highway.

At the Kona airport, they watched the agricultural inspector open bags, examine their contents, then slap on an orange stamp. When Beth reached the head of the line, she joked that she hoped the inspector would look through her luggage carefully. "I saw some bugs I wouldn't want to take back."

"Where you headed?" said the inspector.

"O'Hare."

"Lady," he said, "those bugs don't *want* to go to Chicago. . . . Taking back any food? . . . Any plants?" She shook her head.

"Now let's see." He opened a suitcase and Link's books toppled onto the floor.

Link picked them up. "Planning a course on modern lit, I see. Where's *By Faith Alone*?"

"In my carry-on. I'm going to start it on the plane."

Arm in arm, they walked about the airport, enjoying the air of revelry. High-spirited souvenir hunters trying on kukui nut necklaces. A jolly polka group playing "Hawaiian War Dance" on their accordions. They pressed through, listening to the din of travel conversation. "Did you get the pineapple?" "Daddy, are we going to take the private plane?" And overriding the noise and excitement, the brilliant afternoon sun embracing everyone, suffusing everything with color.

"After all this," Beth gestured around her, "life will seem very drab."

"I see you haven't read your Osumi today," said Link.

Beth admitted she had been remiss and asked what cheer Osumi offered.

Link brought out a scrap of paper. " 'Yes,' " he writes, " 'life is often colorless and monotonous. Every day we get up, eat, go to work, then come home and go to bed again. But life is what we make it. Cheer up, friends. Pull yourselves together.' Not exactly *New York Times* op-ed material."

"Maybe it should be," said Beth. "I'm going to miss the Reverend Osumi."

"And I," said Link, "am going to miss you." He took her in his arms. The polka group moved into "It Happened in Hawaii."

Twice Beth's plane was announced. The third time they drew apart and walked toward the terminal.

"I'd like to see you next week," said Link. "Better yet, tomorrow. But I can't make it till April. I'll be in Chicago then, giving a talk. Can I see you?"

"Of course." Go for it.

"Good," he said, taking her in his arms again. "I have some ideas we can discuss. I think I know how Dorothea can find fulfill-ment—and no longer be in a subservient position."

"There are some men," she said breathlessly, her face against his shirt, "who would have said I talked too much about *Middlemarch*."

"Never," he said, following with a kiss to end all kisses, a kiss that Bogie and Ingrid might have envied, a kiss to remember on cold winter mornings and soft summer afternoons.

The plane lifted off. She waved until Link disappeared from view. He'd have to run to make his flight to New York. Then they were over the water and the attendant was taking drink orders. She looked through the magazines—they were all in Japanese. Inside her bag was a crossword and *By Faith Alone.* She hesitated—took the crossword.

It was dark when the plane took off from Honolulu a few hours later. The attendants, who had discarded flowered silks for uni-forms, grimly went about their tasks. "The time in Chicago is now 1:00 A.M.," the pilot announced. "The temperature," he said, as everyone reset their watches, "is five degrees below zero. The windchill is forty below zero." The ensuing groans were like a mourner's dirge—requiem for a holiday.

Beth thought about the bitter winds off the lake, the snow bit-ing into her face as she fought her way across the quadrangles. Then she thought about seeing her colleagues, catching up on the latest campus intrigues. She thought about meeting her new stu-dents and how she planned to approach *Middlemarch* with them. She took out a notebook and lost herself in filling its pages with ideas.

The movie came on. Beth turned on her light and looked at *By Faith Alone.* On its cover a group of people, the men in dress uni-form, the women in evening gowns and ankle-strap platforms. In the background, Big Ben, small hand pointed at seven, big hand pointed at just before eight—1939? she wondered. She opened the book and read the first sentences.

When he opened his eyes, he saw rows of books, leather bindings shining in the firelight, walls stacked floor to ceiling with landscape paintings, floors covered with English carpet overlaid with worn Oriental rugs—and across the room a steel file cabinet, and a beautiful woman, rifling its contents. "My dear," she said. "You're awake, and about time too."

He tried to remember who he was.

Not a bad beginning. She settled in for the flight.